THE DEAD KID DID IT

SPINETINGLERS

#10

THE DEAD KID DID IT

M. T. COFFIN

AN AVON CAMELOT BOOK

THE DEAD KID DID IT is an original publication of Avon Books. This work has never before appeared in book form.

AVON BOOKS
A division of
The Hearst Corporation
1350 Avenue of the Americas
New York, New York 10019

Copyright © 1996 by George Edward Stanley
Excerpt from *Fly By Night* copyright © 1996 by Kathleen Duey
Published by arrangement with the author
Library of Congress Catalog Card Number: 95-96066
ISBN: 0-380-78314-2
RL: 4.9

First Avon Camelot Printing: June 1996

CAMELOT TRADEMARK REG. U.S. PAT. OFF. AND IN OTHER COUNTRIES, MARCA REGISTRADA, HECHO EN U.S.A.

Printed in the U.S.A.

OPM   10 9 8 7 6 5 4 3 2 1

I burst into our classroom and screamed, "I just opened my locker, and this dead kid tried to pull me inside!"

For a few seconds, everyone looked stunned. Then the kids all started to laugh, but our teacher, Ms. Kienzle, said, "Dunning Healy, take your seat, and if you ever try that again, you'll be sent to the principal's office. We don't play practical jokes here at Wilson Elementary School."

I started to protest, because it wasn't a joke, but the look on Ms. Kienzle's face told me that you didn't talk back to teachers here, either.

In the two days that I had been at Wilson Elementary School, I had already found out that there were a lot of things that were different from my last school. There, we only had *one* sixth grade teacher. At Wilson, we had two, Ms. Kienzle and Mr. Jones, and we alternated between their classes, because the principal, Mr. Crabtree, was trying to get us ready for junior high school.

That was the reason we had lockers, too, just like we would next year, except that for some reason mine had a dead kid in it.

But who was going to believe me now? I wondered. I doubted if anyone in this room would.

When I enrolled, I was assigned the only remaining seats in Ms. Kienzle's and Mr. Jones's classes. They were both right in the middle of the room. Now I was completely surrounded by fifty eyes staring at me, wondering, I was sure, what kind of weirdo I was.

I knew what had happened to me, though. I wasn't making this up.

It all started because I had forgotten to bring my free-reading book to class. When I told Ms. Kienzle about it, she said, "Well, you're new and you're not used to our routine, so yes, you may go out to your locker and get it, but from now on, Dunning, remember that we have free reading on Thursday mornings."

I assured her that I wouldn't forget again.

I left the classroom, rounded the corner, found my locker in the middle of the section, turned the combination lock, and opened the door. I thought

I had put my free-reading book on top of my other books, but I didn't see it anywhere.

So I took out all of my schoolbooks and set them on the floor. My free-reading book had fallen to the back of my locker. I reached in to get it, and that's when it happened.

This dead kid grabbed me and tried to pull me inside!

I knew he was dead, because he looked just like all those dead people I'd seen in horror movies. I know what I'm talking about, too, since those are the only kind I ever rent.

I had to struggle hard to get out of the kid's grasp—he was really strong—and it took me a couple of minutes, but I finally pulled loose and slammed the locker door. I grabbed my book, then I started running as fast as I could back to my classroom to tell Ms. Kienzle. I mean, after all, when you go to school, you don't expect to be pulled into your locker by a dead kid. I just knew she'd do something about it.

Bad idea.

Now all I wanted to do was disappear.

It seemed to take Ms. Kienzle forever to start talking again, so that all those eyes wouldn't be staring at me, but she finally did.

"Class, I'll give you twenty minutes to read in your free-reading books, then we'll have a short period of time when you may each summarize what you read."

I swallowed hard. Oh, no! I couldn't believe it. When was this nightmare going to end? I had brought one of my favorite books from home, *The Cemetery under the School,* but I didn't want to talk about it in class. I thought we were just going to read them. Now I'd have to tell everyone that I was reading a book about a school that had been built on top of a cemetery and how all kinds of weird things were happening because of it. I'd never live it down. Everyone would believe that all I ever did was think about dead people.

I had already seen some of the books the other kids were reading: *Little Women, The Red Badge of Courage,* and *Light in the Forest.* Oh, well, I thought. At least I was reading what I wanted to. Those kids were probably reading their books to try to impress Ms. Kienzle.

I opened the book to the first page. I'd read it so many times I could probably quote it word for word, but I never got tired of reading it.

I had just finished reading the first paragraph when I felt someone poke me in the back.

Oh, oh, I thought. It's started. I just knew that whoever it was, was going to make some smart remark about what I had done, so I ignored it.

But the poking continued.

I took a deep breath and slowly turned around, ready to confront whoever it was.

It was a girl. She gave me a quick smile and handed me a note. Then she looked back down at her book.

I turned around quickly and looked to see if Ms. Kienzle had seen what had happened, but she hadn't, so I unfolded the note and read: I BELIEVE YOU. I USED TO HAVE YOUR LOCKER. THE SAME THING HAPPENED TO ME, TOO. LET'S TALK AFTER SCHOOL. KIM BARSTOW.

I gulped. I knew I hadn't been making it up, but until this very moment I was sure that everyone else in the class had thought I was.

I wrote OKAY at the bottom of the note and then, without looking around, put my hand in the aisle and handed the note back to her. She took it.

I heard her opening it.

Well, maybe things were going to work out all right after all, I thought. I could hardly wait to talk to Kim Barstow after school.

2

Unfortunately, Kim had to take a makeup test, so we couldn't talk right after school. I wasn't sure what I was going to do now, but I knew I didn't want to go home. I had to talk to her about what had happened to me. I just couldn't wait until tomorrow.

But I didn't want to hang around outside the classroom or in the halls or on the school grounds, either. Since Ms. Kienzle had made me talk about my book first, because I was the new kid and because everyone wanted to know what I read in my free time, I was sure the other kids would be waiting so they could make smart remarks about how all I ever did was think about dead people.

"How long will it take?" I whispered to Kim when she and I and Ms. Kienzle were the only people left in the room.

"About fifteen minutes. It's math. I'm very good in math."

I suddenly brightened. Maybe this day wasn't going to be such a bummer after all. Not only had Kim agreed to help me with my locker problem, but she could probably also help me with math, which was my weakest subject.

"Go straight to your locker," she whispered. "I'll meet you there in fifteen minutes."

My locker! I thought. I didn't want to hang around my locker for fifteen minutes, either. Somebody would see me and, after they had made their smart remarks, dare me to open it. There was no way I'd ever do that again.

Before I could say anything, though, Ms. Kienzle handed Kim the makeup test and told me to leave, so I started dragging my book bag out of the room. It was too heavy to carry, because it had every one of my schoolbooks in it.

That was another problem I had to solve. What was I going to do with all these books? I had every book for all my subjects. I guess I should be thankful that I had taken them out of my locker, because at least I would have them when I needed them, but I didn't want to take them all home with me, and I certainly didn't want to put them back inside my locker and take another chance on the dead kid grabbing my arm.

I shook my head in disgust. Why did Wilson Elementary School make you change classes and use lockers when you got to the sixth grade? Why couldn't they just wait for junior high school?

I was now standing about five feet from my locker, just looking at it, and all of a sudden, I had the strangest feeling. Had I just been making all this up? I wondered. My teachers were always telling me that I had a very vivid imagination. Maybe that's what this was: my imagination. I mean, yeah, Kim had written me that note and all, but maybe that was just a joke, too. I hadn't really paid any attention to Kim before today. How did I know I could trust her?

Or maybe it was just a poster I had been looking at. Maybe the last kid who had had the locker had pasted a picture of a monster at the back and I just *thought* it was trying to get me.

I'd read about things like that, where people were so scared, their minds convinced them that all sorts of weird things were happening when, actually, it was all in their heads. But why hadn't I seen it before today? Maybe someone had just put it there as a practical joke. Sure! That's what it was!

But what a grip that kid had! It was so powerful!

I sighed. Of course, maybe I had just gotten

my wrist stuck on something inside the l
and I only *thought* it was somebody pulling
inside.

I thought about Kim again. Should I really
wait and find out what she had to tell me? That
note had seemed so sincere. Was she telling the
truth, though? Was this whole thing a setup just
to make me look even more foolish than I did
now?

I bet that was it! It was a setup! Kim had probably put the poster there.

Kim knew she had this makeup test after
school, so why did she tell me to meet her if it
weren't a joke? In fact, Ms. Kienzle was probably
in on it, too. I bet if I sneaked back to the classroom and looked in, everyone would be there,
laughing at me and planning all the practical
jokes they were going to play all year.

I was really getting angry now! Why had we
moved to this stupid town in the first place? If
that dumb Mr. Hooker hadn't died, Dad wouldn't
have been hired to replace him!

I dragged my book bag over to the locker and
stood staring at it. It was just an ordinary metal
locker in the middle of a row of other ordinary
metal lockers. Where did I get the crazy idea that
there was a dead kid inside who was trying to get

me? Dunning Healy, you are so dumb sometimes! You've really made a mess of this day.

I sighed again. "I'm going home," I muttered.

But first I was going to put all of these dumb books back inside my dumb locker. There was no way I was going to carry them all the way home, dead kid or no dead kid!

I turned the combination lock and opened the door.

But I stood back, just in case.

There was no poster pasted on the back wall, so how could I have seen that horrible dead face? Maybe I'd been making that up, too. Maybe that face was one I had seen in a movie and all of a sudden when I got scared it came to mind.

Then I noticed a couple of guys coming slowly down the hall. They were looking at me and whispering. I didn't remember seeing them in my class, but I could tell from the way they were acting that the story of what had happened to me this morning had made it all over school.

They kept walking slower and slower. I knew they were waiting for me to put my books inside the locker to see what would happen. Actually, they had fear on their faces, so that probably meant they were fourth or fifth graders. They usually believe whatever sixth graders tell them.

Finally, they were opposite my locker.

10

"Are you Dunning Healy?" one of them ventured.

"Yes. What do you want?"

"Did that really happen to you this morning?"

"Did *what* really happen to me this morning?" I absolutely wasn't going to give anything away.

The other kid said, "You know, the thing with that *dead* kid. Did he really try to pull you into the locker?"

I just looked at them for a minute. They were serious about this, I could tell. They didn't think it was some kind of a joke.

I looked around to see if anybody was watching us, but there was nobody else in the hall.

"Yeah, it did," I said.

They both shivered.

"I wouldn't make something like that up," I continued. I checked again to see if anybody was looking. Nobody.

"Do you think it'll happen again?" one of the kids asked.

I shrugged.

Then I suddenly had a great idea! With these two guys here, I could put my books inside my locker. If the dead kid tried to pull me inside, then I'd have witnesses who could pull me out. I'd also have two more people who believed me, and if I knew fourth and fifth graders, it would be all over school tomorrow that Dunning Healy really did have a dead kid in his locker.

"You boys need to be outside, if you're not making up work."

I turned and saw one of the other teachers walking toward us. The two guys hurried on down the hall.

Foiled again, I thought. "I was just putting my books inside my locker," I told her. "I'm new, and I was having trouble remembering the combination."

"Aren't you the Healy boy?" she asked.

I nodded. "Yes, ma'am."

She gave me a pitying look. "I wish there were something I could do to help you, young man," she said. Then she headed down another hallway.

I gulped. There was no way I'd ever survive this year at Wilson Elementary School.

I looked at my watch. Fifteen minutes had already passed, and Kim still wasn't there. It had just been a practical joke after all. I had to admit that I really was a little bit disappointed. Oh, well, what's the difference? I decided. I took the books that I didn't need tonight out of my book bag and put them inside my locker.

But while my hand was still there, it was gripped hard by skeleton fingers, and I was suddenly being pulled inside.

12

"Help me!" I screamed. "Help me!"

I had fallen to the floor, and I was slowly being dragged headfirst into darkness behind my locker.

"Help me!" I screamed again. This time my words had a strange echo to them, as though my head were inside a cavern. The dead kid had me, and his grip on my wrist was like being held in a vice!

Then, suddenly, I was being pulled backward out of the locker. I felt like the rope in a tug-of-war.

Then, just as suddenly, I was going forward again!

What's going on here? I wondered.

I wanted to scream, but I could hardly breathe. There was this really awful odor in the darkness.

The tug-of-war went on for what seemed like forever. The dead kid would pull me forward; then whoever had my feet would pull me backward.

Finally, whoever had my feet gave a big yank and pulled me out of the locker and onto the floor.

The locker door slammed shut.

I looked up and through a haze saw the grinning face of Kim Barstow.

"The dead kid again?"

I managed to nod.

"Figures." She helped me up. "Sorry I was late. I couldn't do those math problems as well as I thought I could."

I sighed and leaned heavily against the closed door of my locker. I didn't want to hear that. I had been counting on Kim's helping me with my math. If she couldn't do that, then how could she help me with my locker problem?

"We need to talk about this on the way home," Kim said.

Before we left school, I asked Mrs. Cuttahee, the principal's secretary, if I could use her telephone to call home.

"You're Dunning Healy, aren't you?"

I swallowed hard and nodded. It really wasn't a question, though; it was a statement, and I was sure she meant: You're the one telling that story about the dead kid trying to pull you into the locker, aren't you?

She kept looking at me, like she was trying to read my mind to see what kind of a lunatic they had at Wilson Elementary School, so I said, "It's true! It really happened!"

That made her blink. She turned away but said, "Well, hurry. We can't tie up the telephone on personal business."

Mom finally answered on the tenth ring. I knew she was home, but she had been outside planting some chrysanthemums. Mom loves flowers, and she plants whichever ones will bloom during the different seasons.

"Sorry, Dunning, but I had to wash my hands before I could pick up the telephone."

"I'm going to Kim's house, Mom, so I'll be late."

"*Kim?*"

"She's in the sixth grade, too."

"Oh? What do her parents do, Dunning?"

I turned away so Kim couldn't see me. "I don't know, Mom. I didn't ask. What difference does it make?"

"Dunning, you know I don't like you associating with people who don't have the same values as we do."

I let out a big sigh. My parents are so sure that one of these days I'm going to make friends with a drug dealer that they drive me crazy. I know how to pick my friends. "Look, it's kind of complicated. Something happened today, and Kim is going to help me with it."

That was the wrong thing to say. "What happened, Dunning? Are you in trouble? If you are, we'll get you the best lawyer in town. Your father has already made some contacts."

Mrs. Cuttahee had begun tapping her foot. I turned back to Kim. "What's your telephone number?"

16

"555-3221."

I repeated the number to Mom. "I'll explain everything when I get home. If you need me before that, then you have Kim's number. Bye." I hung up before she could say anything else.

"Ready?" Kim said.

I nodded. "Thank you," I said to Mrs. Cuttahee. "You're very kind to let me use the telephone, and I apologize for being on the line longer than I should have."

She nodded curtly, but I could tell she was impressed by my politeness. In elementary school, it pays to be friends with the principal's secretary. On more than one occasion, it has saved my life.

Outside, I started to explain the telephone conversation to Kim, but she held up her hand. "Don't try to explain your parents, Dunning. I can't explain mine, either. Your mother probably thinks I'm a drug dealer or something like that, right?"

I nodded. "How did you know?"

She grinned. "I've gone through the same thing myself."

"Well, that's a relief. So tell me what happened when you had my locker."

"Okay. We moved here two months ago, and they assigned that locker to me. It was awful. I

17

had gone to put some books in it, and this dead kid tried to pull me inside."

"That is exactly what happened to me. Did you tell anybody else about it?"

Kim shook her head. "I knew better." She looked at me. "This is your first move, isn't it?"

I nodded. "How can you tell?"

"You're green. You're not streetwise."

"What do you mean?"

"When you've moved around as much as I have, you learn not to tell things until you've figured out how people will react to what you say."

"Well, what did you do about it?"

"I almost wasn't able to do anything, because that dead kid is strong."

"You're telling me!"

"But I finally pulled loose and got the door shut. Then I looked around to see if anyone was watching me, because at first I thought it might be a prank."

"A prank? I'd never thought about that. Do you think it was?"

Kim shook her head. "No, because if it had been a prank, then I would have heard giggling. When people play pranks, they're always around somewhere to see if they worked. They can't stay away. They always give themselves away by giggling. I decided not to say anything about it. I

18

knew that if it had been a prank, sooner or later someone would ask me how I liked my locker and give themselves away. Nobody ever did. So that's when I knew that a dead kid really had tried to pull me inside."

I shivered. "This is so weird."

"You're right. It's so weird that no one would believe you if you told them."

"Why not just get somebody else to open the locker and let it happen to them? That would solve it. That way other people would know."

"I tried that. I had a couple of kids help me with the door, because it does stick a little. They opened it for me and nothing happened. I even asked a kid to put some books into it for me while I wasn't there, because I thought the dead kid only did it if nobody else was around. But the kid was still standing there when I came back."

"Nothing happened?"

"No. Nothing happened. I think it must happen only to new kids."

"How'd you get a new locker?"

"I just told the principal that my locker door stuck and I wanted to change. I was lucky, because they had one extra."

"This is so stupid! Why do we have to have lockers and change classes? I mean, give me a break! We're only in the sixth grade."

"I'm sure you were informed when you enrolled, Dunning, that Wilson Elementary School is preparing you for junior high school. Mr. Crabtree doesn't want it to be a shock when we finally get there."

"I'd rather be shocked than have to keep a dead kid from pulling me into my locker every day."

"I know what you mean." She stopped. "Well, this is where I live."

I didn't want to seem pushy, but I wasn't ready to leave, because we really hadn't come to any decision on how to solve my problem. I needed some serious help to figure out what I was going to do about all of this.

"Nice house," I said and just stood there.

"Want a snack? My dad makes great cookies."

"Sounds good to me. I'd also like to talk some more about my problem. I could really use your advice." People always like to hear that, I knew.

"Come on, then. I think better after I've eaten a couple of chocolate chip cookies."

I followed Kim into her house, where she introduced me to her father, who said hello to me and then handed her a plate of chocolate chip cookies.

When we were in the family room, Kim said, "Dad was laid off a few months ago. He's a chemical engineer. Mom got a job here in Belton, so that's why we're here. Actually, Dad's enjoying

20

being a househusband. He's discovering all these talents he didn't know he had."

"My dad was hired to replace a dead man. That's why we're here."

"It's weird, isn't it, how your life can change so fast. I mean, one morning you wake up, and everything is normal, and by the end of the day, it isn't."

"You're telling me. Mmmm. These are the best chocolate chip cookies I've ever tasted."

"They are, aren't they?"

I reached for a second one and said, "So what am I going to do?"

Kim took another bite of cookie and said, "It's hard. You've got the only locker left, and these lockers are really big deals. Mr. Crabtree used to be the junior high principal, but he just couldn't take it. His one goal in life is to prepare us for junior high, so we won't be swallowed up like he was."

"Junior high sounds awful," I said.

"Actually, I'm looking forward to it, but I do think you have to be prepared. You can't just go in cold."

"Maybe I could leave the books I use in Ms. Kienzle's class in her room and the books that I use in Mr. Jones's class in his room. That way I won't have to use my locker."

"It won't work, Dunning. Some of the other kids have already tried that. Mr. Crabtree wants us to use our lockers. In fact, he makes sure we're using them. There are periodic locker checks."

I was beginning to feel panicky. "I just can't go through this every day, Kim. I just can't fight off the dead kid every time I want to use my locker. One of these days, I'm going to lose, and there's no telling where I'll end up."

Kim took another cookie. "That might be the answer."

I looked at her. "What?"

"Where you'd end up. If we can find out what's on the other side of your locker, then we could attack the problem from that side."

"How could we do that?"

"Well, I'm sure the dead kid doesn't stay behind the back of the locker all the time, just waiting for it to be opened. Surely he knows that it's only going to be opened during the day when we're at school. And besides, he doesn't appear every time it's opened. He has to be someplace else."

"That makes sense."

"So if we could be there at night, then we could check out the locker without something happening to us."

I took a deep breath. "You may have something

there, but I don't like the idea of tempting fate. What if he's waiting behind the door? I mean, he's dead, so he probably doesn't do things like we would. I bet time doesn't mean anything to him. He might even *live* behind the locker."

"Well, we don't have to do anything about this, Dunning, but sooner or later you're going to have to use your locker."

I knew I was beaten. "How'll we get inside the school?"

Kim smiled. I could tell she was looking forward to this. "There's a PTA meeting tonight, so the building will be open."

"There'll be people around, though. That's exactly what we don't want."

"I know that, but when it's over, we'll be inside the school. All we have to do is hide and wait until everyone has left. I know a great place, too. As soon as the janitor has left and turned off the lights, we'll wait a few minutes to make sure the dead kid knows everyone has left. Then we'll check out the locker to see what's behind it."

"It might work. Maybe there's a trapdoor that leads somewhere."

"That's what I think."

I stood up. "I'd better go home. Mom will be wondering what I've been doing. What time does the PTA meeting start?"

"Seven o'clock, but make sure your parents don't come."

When I looked puzzled, Kim added, "If they come, they'll want you to go home with them."

"Oh, yeah."

"Just tell them you're going with me. I'll come by for you at six-fifteen. My parents never go. Mom always works late, and Dad still feels kind of funny when people ask him what he does for a living."

I said good-bye, told Mr. Barstow what a great cookie maker he was, and left Kim's house.

I got lost a couple of times on the way home, because I had never walked to my house from this direction. Thank goodness Belton isn't all that big.

I couldn't believe how crazy things had turned out. I didn't blame people for thinking there was something wrong with me. I mean, it did sound kind of crazy, telling people that there was a dead kid inside my locker and that every time I opened it he tried to pull me inside.

I rubbed my wrist. I wasn't making that part up, I knew. This dead kid was strong—and that frightened me. There was no telling what he'd do to me—*us!*—if he caught me and Kim and there was nobody else around to save us.

I wasn't sure I was doing the right thing, trying to get to the bottom of this, but I couldn't spend all year at Wilson Elementary School avoiding my locker.

Finally, I reached my house and bounded up the front steps. "Mom, I'm home!"

She rushed into the living room, gave me the once-over, and decided, I was sure, that I hadn't gone through some gang initiation. "So you were at Kim's?"

"Yes, and her father makes the best chocolate chip cookies, too."

"Wonderful. So how was the rest of your day?"

"It was great."

"Do you think you're going to like living here in Belton?"

"I think so."

"Well, do you have any homework?"

"No, but I need to go back to school tonight for a PTA meeting."

"Oh, goodness, and I had some other plans for this evening. Oh, well, I guess I can cancel them."

"Oh, no, that's not necessary. Kim said that this wasn't all that important, but that I probably should go, because they might want me to help with some project or something."

"Are you sure?"

"I'm sure. We may go out for pizza afterward, too, if that's all right."

25

"With Kim?"

I nodded.

"Well, I am so thrilled that you've made a good friend the first week of school. That's just wonderful. I can already tell that you're going to have a great school year!"

Yeah, right! I thought. If I can only figure out a way to keep this dead kid from pulling me into my locker every time I open it!

4

Kim came by for me as planned, and I introduced her to Mom and Dad.

"I'll be glad to drive you," Mom said, when she realized we were walking.

"That's all right, Mrs. Healy," Kim said. "It's not far, and I could use the exercise. I ate too many of my dad's chocolate chip cookies this afternoon."

"Dunning told me how good they were. I'll have to get the recipe."

"It's a secret. He'd never give it to you. I could probably get a copy, though, if you really need it."

Mom looked puzzled. "Oh, well, no, that's all right. I was just . . ."

"Well, we'll see you later," I said hurriedly. We had to get out of there before Mom decided that Kim was too weird for me to hang out with.

"Sometimes we go out for pizza after PTA, Mrs. Healy. Is it all right if Dunning comes, too?"

"I think that would be okay, as long as it's not too late. I don't like Dunning to stay out late on a school night."

"I'll be all right, Mom," I said. Gee! I couldn't believe how she was treating me in front of Kim. I almost pulled Kim out the door.

Outside, I said, "Do you really think this is going to work? I mean, what we're talking about here is probably illegal."

"I've given this a lot of thought since this afternoon, Dunning, and no, I don't really think it's illegal."

"I can hardly wait to hear this," I said.

"It's simple. It would only be illegal if we broke into the school after it was locked. I don't think it's against the law if you get locked in a building by mistake."

"Mistake? We're planning this!"

"Well, we don't have to tell anyone what we're doing. We went there for a legitimate reason, to attend a PTA meeting, and we just got locked in, because we were both using the rest room."

"That sounds really phony to me, Kim, that both of us happened to be using the rest room when we were locked in."

Kim stopped. "Dunning, I don't know why you're so worried about this. It's not like we're going to have to explain it to anyone."

28

"I just thought we should have an excuse ready in case we get caught. You never know what's going to happen."

Kim let out a big sigh. "Oh, all right. I'll think of something during the PTA meeting. Just relax, though. You really don't have anything to worry about."

I hated it when anybody said that to me, because every time it had happened before, I'd been involved in a total disaster.

When we finally got to the school, I was surprised at how many cars were parked in front.

"Nobody ever went to PTA meetings at my last school," I said.

"It's good to have a lot of people around when you're planning to hide in the school," Kim said, "because nobody pays that much attention to you."

I started to ask her how she knew that, because it certainly sounded like she'd done it before, but I decided I didn't want to know.

We took our seats at the back of the auditorium just as the program was beginning. It was hot, so there were a lot of big fans blowing, which meant I couldn't hear anything except for crying babies.

"This is the really boring part," Kim said. "They're talking about fund-raisers and deciding

29

whether they want us to sell candy bars or wrapping paper."

"Why should we sell either one?"

"The PTA wants to buy some new playground equipment. Is that dumb or what? I mean, who needs it, right? We'll be out of here in a year, anyway, and I don't want to spend my last year here selling candy bars or wrapping paper so the first, second, and third graders can have new playground equipment. I mean, let them use what we had to use!"

"Can't we protest it or something? I don't want to sell anything, either."

Kim shrugged. "Well, Mr. Crabtree is on our side at least. He wants to use the money for new computers instead of playground equipment. If they won't let him do that, then he might decide we can't sell anything."

Finally, the business meeting was over. We'd be selling candy bars, but we'd decide how to spend the money later. The rest of the program was the kindergarten choir, and it was kind of funny, because these little kids kept wandering around all over the stage, waving to their parents in the audience.

Then finally that was over.

"We need to hide, don't we?" I whispered to Kim.

"Not before we get some refreshments," she replied.

We stood in line and got some cookies and punch. I couldn't believe how many cookies Kim got, not after all the ones she said she had eaten at her house.

I was thirsty, so I got a cup of pineapple punch, which wasn't too bad. At least it was cold.

Then, finally, Kim said, "It's time."

I was glad, because a lot of people had already begun to leave.

I followed Kim out into one of the halls, then down it, until we reached a door. "This leads to the stage," she whispered.

The two of us slipped inside.

Now we were behind the curtain. That was the only thing separating us from the people who were still milling around in the auditorium.

"In here," Kim whispered. She pointed to a door at the back of the stage. "They keep the props and costumes for all the plays in here. Nobody ever checks it."

She opened the door and we stepped inside. It was black as pitch.

I was afraid to move, because I just knew that I'd knock something over and Mr. Crabtree would come running in and find us.

But then Kim produced a little flashlight that

31

lit up the room enough so that we could see what we were doing.

"There's a light, but you can see it under the cracks of the door. You can't see this."

She anticipated my next question.

"I've checked it out before. I never do anything halfway."

I started to ask her why she had hidden in the school before, but I decided I still didn't want to know.

We waited for what seemed like forever, but then Kim suddenly switched off the light and whispered, "Be perfectly still."

I held my breath.

For a few minutes, I didn't hear anything, but then I heard someone moving around on the stage. I began to break out in a cold sweat. The door to the room we were in wasn't locked, so if a person opened it, we'd be found immediately.

I could just picture Mr. Crabtree saying, "Ah hah! I knew it would be you, Dunning Healy. You're expelled!"

Then the footsteps seemed to be getting fainter, and I heard a door close.

Still Kim didn't say anything, but in a few seconds she switched the flashlight back on and started looking at her watch.

Finally, she said, "He's gone."

32

"Who's gone?" I whispered.

"Mr. Whitton, the janitor. I've timed him before. After he leaves the stage area, he checks the other side of the building. Then he leaves by the side door, where his car is parked. It always takes him ten minutes exactly."

This was getting weirder and weirder. How did Kim know all of this? I was beginning to get very suspicious of this whole operation.

"Maybe we should wait another ten minutes," I said when Kim stood up to leave.

"There's no need, Dunning. I have this timed to the last second."

This was sounding more and more like somebody who was planning to rob a bank or something, and I was wondering what else Kim was interested in doing besides seeing what the dead kid was up to.

I had just about decided to ask her when she opened the door. I hadn't realized how stale it had become inside the storage closet. I took a deep breath and followed Kim out onto the stage area.

She led the way to the side door and opened it.

She peered out. "It pays to be careful," she whispered.

Actually, I was still expecting Mr. Crabtree to jump out at us.

33

Kim turned off the flashlight. "I know my way down the hallway. Besides, you can see the light from outside, and I don't want any passing motorists to call the police."

I don't either, I thought.

Finally, we reached the hall where my locker was.

I was beginning to get very nervous. "Are you sure Mr. Crabtree won't just let me switch lockers?" I said. It occurred to me again that the only person I had been talking to about all of this was Kim, and from the way she was acting, I was beginning to wonder again if I could trust her. Maybe she really didn't know what she was talking about.

"He won't, Dunning. You have the last empty locker. I told you how Mr. Crabtree feels about this. It's very important to him that we are prepared to survive in junior high school."

We had now reached my locker.

"Here we are," Kim whispered.

"Why are we whispering?" I whispered.

"We don't know for sure where the dead kid is," Kim said. "If I'm right about all of this, then he knows there's no one in the school, so he's probably gone back to wherever it is he goes when he's not trying to pull new kids into the locker, but you can't be too careful."

34

What I wanted to do was run out of the building and back to my house and never come out again, but I knew that in order to face this year at Wilson Elementary School, I was going to have to take care of this problem. I was going to have to convince this dead kid that he needed to let me put my books in my locker without trying to pull me inside.

"Open the door," Kim whispered.

I looked at her. *"Me?"*

"It's your locker, Dunning. You need to open it."

I gulped. For some reason I thought Kim was going to open it. I thought that was the reason she had come along with me.

"Well, uh, okay," I managed to say.

Slowly, I moved my hands toward the lock. I began to picture the dead kid waiting on the other side, holding his breath, ready to grab my wrist and drag me inside.

My hand finally touched the metal locker.

"Ouch!" I cried and jerked away. My heart was pounding.

"What's wrong?" Kim said.

"It shocked me!" I whispered back. My finger still stung.

"It's just static electricity," Kim said. "It won't hurt you."

35

"It stung," I said.

"Dunning, we really don't have all night to do this. If you want to go home and just deal with this in the morning, then that's fine with me. I'm only trying to help you, but I need just a little cooperation from you."

I took a deep breath. "Okay."

I reached out again for the combination lock. It shocked me again, but I gritted my teeth and didn't pull away.

Kim shined the flashlight on it, and I began to turn the combination. It clicked. Then I slowly pulled the door open.

I expected this skeleton hand to reach out and grab me, but I finally had the locker door all the way open and nothing had happened.

Kim and I just stood there for a few minutes, before she finally shined the flashlight inside the locker.

"There must be some way into the locker from behind it. That has to be the way he does it," she said. "He obviously doesn't live *inside* of it."

"Maybe there's a secret door, like they have in old houses," I suggested.

"It has to be something like that," Kim agreed.

"Where would it go, though?"

"That's what we have to find out."

"What's on the other side of this hallway?"

"The cafeteria."

"The *cafeteria?* Do you think the dead kid lives in the cafeteria?"

Kim thought for just a minute. "You know something? That would make sense. The food at this school is just awful. Maybe the cafeteria cooks are all dead and this is one of their kids who's causing the problem."

"If that's true, then we're in serious trouble."

"I just thought of something else, too," Kim said. "Maybe this is just some kid who died from eating the food in the cafeteria and he wants to tell someone what happened and the cooks won't let him."

I wasn't quite sure if Kim was serious or not, but it all sort of made sense in a really creepy way.

"I'll hold the flashlight while you press on the back of the locker and see what happens," Kim said.

Since I hadn't been dragged in immediately after I had opened the locker door, I was beginning to get a little bolder. I wanted this to be over, too, and I knew we didn't have all night to take care of it.

I put both of my hands against the back of the locker and pushed.

Nothing happened.

I pushed harder.

Still nothing happened.

"Maybe there's a latch on the other side that the dead kid opens," Kim said.

I hadn't thought about that. "We'll never get in if there is," I said.

I decided to push one more time. I gave it all I had, and the back of my locker opened!

A horrible smell filled the air and made us both gag.

"What is that?" Kim managed to say.

"It smells like something died," I said. Then we looked at each other and realized what that meant.

Holding her nose, Kim moved closer and shined the flashlight into the opening behind the locker. "Look, Dunning!" she cried. "There's a hole here!"

I looked. "Someone's tunneled up from somewhere to right behind my locker. Where do you think it goes?"

"That's what we need to find out," Kim said, putting one foot into my locker. "Come on!"

5

I just stood there, stunned, as I watched Kim disappear into the black hole that was behind my locker.

"Hurry up, Dunning!" Her voice was an echo. "We don't have all night!"

Against my better judgment, I stepped into my locker and crawled in after her.

Kim was a few feet ahead of me, but her flashlight was doing a good job of lighting up the tunnel. At first we were crawling on our hands and knees, so Kim had to hold the flashlight in her mouth, but gradually the tunnel got bigger, and it wasn't long before we could actually stand up.

"Where do you think this leads to?" I asked.

"We're going down, I know that for sure," Kim said.

I was shaking, but I couldn't tell if it was because I was scared or because I was cold. "I'm freezing," I managed to say.

"Me, too. I wish I'd brought a jacket."

Along the sides of the tunnel, there were large roots that looked like arms. They seemed to be reaching out at us, and I was just sure that any minute one of them would wrap around my throat.

It kept getting colder, and the awful smell, mixed with wet earth, was almost more than I could stand.

Finally, we reached the end of the tunnel and came into a large opening.

"What is this place?"

Kim shined the flashlight around. "I don't know." She started forward and I followed.

For several minutes, we couldn't see anything. Then the flashlight picked up a casket. The lid was open.

"I think it's a cemetery," Kim whispered.

I suddenly remembered my free-reading book! "With one casket? That's not much of a cemetery."

"I wonder why the lid's open?"

"I'm not sure I want to know."

"It probably belongs to the dead kid," Kim said.

"If this is a cemetery, why is there only one person buried here?"

"That's what we're here to find out, Dunning. Come on."

"Wait, Kim. If it is the dead kid, then he'll probably grab us and never let us go."

"Remember that there are two of us. If he grabs you, then I'll run for help."

"Oh, thanks a lot. By the time you get back, it'll be too late."

"Hello? Dead kid?" Kim called. "Are you there?"

"What are you doing?" I hissed.

"Do you have a better idea? I mean, how else do you contact a dead person? We don't have time for a seance."

"You're right. I guess that's as good a way as any."

"Hello! Dead kid?" Kim called again.

Suddenly, the lid of the casket slammed shut, causing us both to jump several feet into the air.

Then a skeleton hand touched my shoulder and I screamed.

Kim and I both turned around.

The flashlight was shining in the dead kid's skeleton face!

For a couple of seconds, Kim and I just stood there, then we both started running.

The dead kid started after us.

It didn't take us long to realize that we were trapped in the huge underground room.

41

Finally, the dead kid shouted, "Stop! Please! I can't run anymore!"

For some reason, Kim and I stopped.

The dead kid was standing just a few feet away, facing us. Kim kept the flashlight in his face.

"Would you mind not doing that?" the dead kid said.

"Do you promise not to chase us again?" Kim said.

"I wasn't chasing you. I was only trying to keep up with you. You were the ones who started running first. If you hadn't started running, I wouldn't have been running."

"Well, what do you want?" I was absolutely amazed that I was underground somewhere talking to a dead kid.

"I need your help."

"Well, you certainly have a funny way of trying to get it," Kim said.

"What do you mean?" he asked.

"You know," I said. "You tried to pull both of us into the locker."

"I'm sorry. It's just that I was desperate. I've been trying for fifty years to get somebody to help me."

"*Fifty years?*"

"Yes. It hasn't been easy, either. Nobody I ever

42

approached would do anything about my problem. They wouldn't tell anyone that they had talked to me."

"You mean you've been talking to kids in this school for fifty years?"

The dead kid nodded. "It was only when Mr. Crabtree put in those lockers that I was able to dig a tunnel up into the school and still keep myself hidden during the day. I thought if I could just get somebody into the tunnel and show them what my problem was, they'd help me."

"You never got anybody down here before?" I asked.

The dead kid shook his head. "No. Years ago, though, I'd sometimes just show up at night, when kids would be in the school for different events and things, and I'd try to talk to them, but they'd all run away, and I didn't want to chase them all over town."

I pinched myself to see if I was asleep. I couldn't believe what I was hearing.

"I'm just lucky that you two decided to come down to the tunnel yourself, because now I can show you what my problem is."

Kim looked at me. "Well, all right, I guess that since we're already here, we might as well listen to what you have to say, but there'd better not be any funny stuff."

43

"I promise," the dead kid said.

"By the way," I said, "what's your name?"

The dead kid had started walking toward his casket. "Jonathan."

"What are you doing, Jonathan?" I called.

"I'm going to show you what I need your help with."

Kim looked at me and shrugged. "Why not?"

We followed Jonathan over to his casket.

"Here it is," Jonathan said.

"Here what is?" Kim said.

"My casket. I need your help to get it moved."

"Moved?" I said. "What are you talking about?"

"It's my own fault, really. I was out haunting the town when they moved the cemetery."

"Moved the cemetery?" Kim said.

"Yes, we're in an old cemetery. The townspeople moved it, so they could build this elementary school building, but, well, I'd been having arguments with my parents, and I decided that I'd just go haunting for a few days on my own. I didn't know they wouldn't be here when I got back, but when I did, they were all gone. I guess they didn't move my casket because there wasn't anybody inside it."

This wasn't making much sense to me. "You mean you were buried here with your parents? What happened?"

44

"We were all killed in a train accident fifty years ago. It was me and my parents and my sister, Josie. Josie was a good kid. She always stayed in her casket. I just couldn't stand that. I had to get out from time to time."

"Why don't you just go where they are? Do you have to have your casket?"

"Oh, yes. I have to have my casket to sleep in. I just couldn't go without it. I mean, there are dead people who just sleep on the ground, but I'm not one of them. I've been waiting for fifty years for somebody to rebury me in my casket."

"That's what you want us to do?" I asked.

Jonathan nodded. "We dead people can't move big things like this. We can haunt people and scare them, but we really can't move things around, no matter what you've seen in the movies."

"You mean you want us to dig up the ground and then carry your casket to the cemetery where your parents are buried?"

"Well, actually, it's a bit more complicated than that. You see, my cemetery is *under* the school." He looked up. "We're standing under Mrs. Gillingham's fifth grade classroom. We'll have to take it up that way, I'm afraid. We'll have to dig a hole in her floor and then use ropes to lift the casket up that way."

45

Kim looked at me. "Dunning, this is just like the book you're reading in Ms. Kienzle's class!"

"I know." I turned back to Jonathan. "Couldn't we just carry it out some other way?"

"Oh, no, no, no, no!" Jonathan said. "These reburials have to be done just right. You have to dig up the ground above where the casket was actually buried, lift it out, and then move it to the new burial site. It has to be done just right."

"We can't dig up the fifth grade classroom," I said. "That's nuts!"

"So you're not going to help me after all? Is that what you're saying?"

"I guess it is!" Kim said.

I could tell that Jonathan was getting really angry.

"We'd like to help you, we really would," I said hurriedly. "It's just that what you're asking us to do is impossible."

Jonathan stomped his foot. "I absolutely refuse to wait another fifty years to be reburied! You will not leave here until you've promised to help me."

I looked over at Kim. "We promise," I said. "Now, we'd better be going."

"Yeah, we promise. See you later."

We started walking away.

46

"I certainly hope I can trust you," Jonathan called to us.

"Oh, you can trust us, all right," Kim said under her breath. "You can trust us to forget about this."

"What?" Jonathan called.

"Nothing," I said.

We were walking a little bit faster now. The flashlight had picked up the opening to the tunnel.

"Move it!" Kim whispered.

I started walking faster. I really did feel bad about this, because Jonathan honestly didn't seem all that bad, but there was no way we could dig up one of the fifth grade classrooms to pull his casket out and then rebury it somewhere else.

We had finally reached the opening to the tunnel.

"Promise?" Jonathan said.

I jumped. He was right behind us and his cold breath caused shivers to go down my spine.

"Yes! Yes! Yes!" Kim said.

We were into the tunnel now, and Jonathan was right behind us. "I repeat. I will not wait another fifty years under this school for someone to rebury me."

"I understand that," I said. "I don't blame you."

"We'll do what we can," Kim said.

47

We had now reached the part of the tunnel where we had to crawl on our hands and knees.

"I mean it!" Jonathan shouted.

"We'll talk to Mr. Crabtree," Kim said. "He's a very understanding principal."

We were now crawling as fast as we could, but Jonathan was crawling behind us.

"Yeah, he probably won't mind at all if we dig up one of the fifth grade classrooms," I said.

"Here it is!" Kim cried.

We had reached my locker. Kim had pulled the trapdoor open and was scrambling into it.

I followed her. "We'll be in touch!" I said to Jonathan.

"Okay. I'm really glad you're going to help me. I kind of miss my parents, you know? After all, it's been a long time."

I crawled through the locker and slammed the outside door.

"Oh, man, that was close!" Kim said. "Let's get out of here."

I was trembling. "Do you think he'll follow us?"

"I don't think so. He thinks we're going to do what he asked us to."

"Do you think we should?"

"Get real, Dunning. I can just see us going up to Mr. Crabtree and telling him we need to dig up Mrs. Gillingham's fifth grade classroom to help

48

Jonathan get his casket out. He'd kick us out of school for sure."

"I know, but I think he really misses his parents, Kim."

"Forget it, Dunning," Kim said. "Come on. We need to get home before our parents start wondering where we were and call the police."

I didn't say anything else until we were almost two blocks from the school. "You know, we haven't solved my locker problem yet. What am I going to do about that?"

"Stall."

"Stall?"

"Yeah, just tell Jonathan that you're doing the best you can, but that it'll take time. He'll have to believe you. If you can stall for eight or nine months, then it won't be your problem anymore. We'll be in junior high school and somebody else can worry about it."

"That's not much of a solution, Kim."

"It's the only thing I can think of. Here's where I turn off. Can you find your way home?"

"Yeah. Sure. I'll see you in the morning."

I wasn't sure I could actually find our house, but I really wanted to be alone. I didn't feel good about going back on my promise to Jonathan. He was really counting on us to help him move his casket. There had to be some solution.

I finally found our house.

Mom and Dad were in the living room.

"Well, I was just about to call the police!" Mom said. "Where have you been?"

"What happened to you?" Dad said, looking at my clothes.

"Oh, it was dark, and I stumbled and fell."

"Well, get them off and get ready for bed. Tomorrow's a school day."

For once, I didn't argue.

I needed to think, too. I had a big problem. I didn't think I could stall Jonathan for nine months. If I didn't find a way to rebury him and his casket, I was sure that he'd pull me into my locker and nobody would ever see me again!

The next morning, when I got to school, I really didn't want to open my locker, because I had no idea what would happen. I kept thinking that Jonathan might have changed his mind and would be waiting to pull me inside. If that happened again, the kids would all laugh and think I was being funny, and I was sure they wouldn't try to pull me out. I waited until the hall was clear, and then I slowly opened the locker door.

When I had the door all the way open and I thought I was going to be all right, the back of the locker swung open and there was Jonathan.

I started to slam the door shut, but he said, "Good morning, Dunning."

"Good morning," I managed to say.

"Well, today's the day, isn't it?"

"What do you mean?"

"Today's the day we move my casket so I can be reburied."

I just looked at him. "I don't think so," I said.

"What do you mean?" I could tell he was getting angry.

"Well, look, it's not easy, you know. First I have to talk to Mr. Crabtree, to get his permission to dig up the floor in Mrs. Gillingham's fifth grade classroom. Then we have to dig up the floor, which is going to take some time, because it's all concrete and stuff like that, probably, and then after we get it dug up, we'll have to . . ."

"Okay, okay, I understand. I didn't think it would really be today, but I was hoping." Jonathan looked at me. "You're telling me the truth, aren't you?"

I shuddered. "Of course. Why wouldn't I be telling you the truth?"

"Oh, I can think of lots of reasons."

"I said I'd help you, didn't I?"

"Yes, you did, but I thought maybe you had changed your mind."

"No."

"Good. I'm afraid that if you had, I would get very angry, and there's no telling what I'd do."

"What do you mean?"

"I decided last night that it has to be now. I'm tired of waiting around."

52

"Can't you just go to the cemetery where your family is and *share* one of their caskets? Do you have to have your own?"

Jonathan laughed. "Oh, Dunning, Dunning! You certainly don't have many dead friends, do you?"

"Well, no, not really."

"You don't share caskets. That's just not done. If you don't have your own casket, then you're just not wanted in a cemetery. You're sort of looked down on. I'm an embarrassment to my parents and to my sister. They don't even want me hanging around the cemetery. I seldom go over there anymore. Actually, I guess it's been about twenty-five years."

"Really?"

"Yes, really, but I'm tired of waiting, so I want you to get the ball rolling today!"

I gulped. "Today?"

"Yes, today!"

"I'll try, but you'll have to be patient."

Jonathan didn't say anything. He just shut the back of the locker.

Just then the second bell rang. I grabbed my books and raced to my class. The bell stopped ringing just before I got to the room.

Ms. Kienzle looked up and watched me take

my seat. "Would you care to explain your tardiness, Dunning?"

"Uh, no, I, well, was just getting something out of my locker. I'm still having trouble with the door."

The girl in front of me raised her hand.

Ms. Kienzle turned. "Yes, Jessica?"

"When I walked by Dunning's locker just a few minutes ago, Ms. Kienzle, he was talking to it."

Several kids started snickering.

Ms. Kienzle blinked. "Is there a point to your story, Jessica?"

"Yes. I don't like sitting by people who talk to their lockers," Jessica said.

"You'll be just fine, Jessica. There are no other seats in the room," Ms. Kienzle said. "Now, everyone, open your readers to page twelve."

I breathed a sigh of relief that Ms. Kienzle either hadn't believed what Jessica had said or had decided not to pursue it. I'd have to watch it, though. I was sure that Jessica wouldn't give up.

I tried to keep my mind on the short story we were reading, but I didn't have much luck.

After reading, we had science with Mr. Jones, which meant I had to get my science book out of my locker.

Jonathan was waiting for me.

"How's it going? Have you talked to Mr. Crabtree yet?"

"No," I whispered. "I haven't had time."

"When are you going to do it?"

"Listen," I whispered, "I can't talk to you. Someone has already told everybody that I talk to my locker!" Then I closed the door before he could say anything.

When I turned around, Jessica Wipple was looking at me with a smile on her face. I knew she could hardly wait to tell Mr. Jones that I'd been talking to my locker.

But Mr. Jones gave us a pop quiz, so she didn't get the chance.

I was a zombie the rest of the day, because all I could think about was having to explain what I was doing to Jonathan every time I opened the locker. It wouldn't be long before I ran out of excuses, and there was no telling what he would do then.

But when I opened my locker to put my music book back in and get out my English book, Jonathan wasn't there. I couldn't believe my luck. I quickly shut the door before he could make an appearance.

When I turned around, Jessica was watching me, so I just smiled and said, "You have the weirdest imagination, Jessica!"

After English, Kim and I headed for the cafeteria.

We got our trays and found a table in the corner away from most of the kids in our class. They seemed interested in talking about other things, so that was fine with me.

"Were you really talking to your locker, Dunning?" Kim asked.

"Of course not! I was talking to Jonathan."

Kim looked surprised. "Really? He didn't try to pull you inside?"

"No. He thinks we're going to rebury him."

"Well, that's impossible, and you know it, so you just need to keep stringing him along."

"I can't do it, Kim. I'm already exhausted, just coming up with excuses today. I'll never last through the end of the year."

"Mace."

"What?"

"Maybe you can get a can of Mace."

"What for?"

"Well, my mother has one. She keeps it so she can spray it in the face of anyone who tries to attack her."

"And this affects me how?"

"Every time you open your locker, you could have the can of Mace handy, and when Jonathan

56

tries to grab you, you can spray the Mace. He'd get the message after a while."

"Mace may work on live people, but who's to say if it'll work on dead people."

Kim thought about that for a moment. "You may have a point there."

"Actually, I really do wish we could find a way to help him. That would be the simplest solution."

"I don't think tearing up the floor of Mrs. Gillingham's fifth grade classroom is a simple solution," Kim said.

She was right, of course. "Do you think your mother will let me borrow her Mace? I guess I could give it a try."

"Probably. Since we moved to Belton, she hasn't thought much about attackers. It's a pretty safe place. It's nothing like L.A. at all. I'll ask her."

"Actually, I was thinking about asking Mr. Crabtree, anyway. All he could say is no."

"Well, yes, that's true, but he could also think you were weirder than he had originally thought you were."

I sighed. "True."

"Maybe you just need to tell Jonathan the truth," Kim said. "Maybe if you level with him, he'll understand. After all, what he's asking is impossible."

I didn't believe that for a minute. "I'll think about it."

I continued to be a zombie through the rest of my classes.

Each time I went to the locker, Jonathan was waiting for me. At the end of sixth hour, when I went to my locker, I said, "I'm going to talk to Mr. Crabtree now. I'll let you know what he has to say, but you'll have to accept it, no matter what."

"Who says?"

"I say. If Mr. Crabtree won't let me do anything, then I can't rebury you. It's that simple."

I closed the door before Jonathan could say anything.

Outside Mr. Crabtree's office, I took two deep breaths and went inside.

Mrs. Cuttahee looked up. "If you want to use the telephone, all right, but just don't tie it up. We have important calls coming into this office all the time."

Yeah, right! I thought. "Actually, I need to talk to Mr. Crabtree."

"Well, you're lucky, because someone just left and the other someone who's supposed to be here hasn't arrived yet, but as soon as that someone does arrive, you'll have to leave, because that someone made an appointment."

"Thank you."

"Go to his door, knock, and then when Mr. Crabtree says, 'Come in,' go in."

I walked over to Mr. Crabtree's door and knocked.

"Come in!"

I opened the door and went in.

"Oh, I was expecting someone who had an appointment. Well, it's all right, Dunning, but when that person arrives you'll have to leave, because that person has an appointment. What may I do for you?"

I thought about trying to set the whole thing up, but I decided that the best thing was just to blurt it out and see what happened.

"Mr. Crabtree, fifty years ago, a boy named Jonathan and his parents and his sister were killed in a train accident and they were buried in a cemetery where this school is now, but before this school was built they moved the cemetery to the other side of town, but Jonathan was having problems with his family, so he wasn't in the cemetery when all of the caskets were dug up and reburied. Well, I guess they dug up his casket, but when they didn't find him in it, they must have just reburied it here, and then they

59

built the school. Well, Jonathan was back in his casket when they built the school and all these years he's been trying to get somebody to dig up his casket again and rebury it in the new cemetery, because, you see, if you don't have a casket then the other dead people don't want you in their cemetery, including his parents and his sister, so he keeps trying to pull me into my locker, so I'll help rebury him, and I even offered to take the casket out a different way, but he said, no, it had to be done right, which means digging up Mrs. Gillingham's fifth grade classroom, because it's over his grave, so can we?"

I hadn't noticed until that moment, but Mr. Crabtree's eyes were going round and round in his head.

"Are you all right, Mr. Crabtree?"

Suddenly, Mr. Crabtree's face got red and the veins on his neck bulged out. He opened his mouth, but nothing came out except sputtering sounds.

"Do you need a drink of water?" I asked. I was beginning to get scared. Now Mr. Crabtree's face was turning purple.

I stood up. I had to get help. The man was obviously not well.

Then the door opened.

Standing there was a policeman! I was sure he had come to arrest me. It was strange, but I was no longer afraid. It was like a peace had settled in on me. Now I didn't have to deal with Jonathan. I was sure that he wouldn't show up where they were going to take me. I held out my hands so the policeman could cuff them.

But he said, "What's wrong with Mr. Crabtree? He looks like he's having a heart attack!"

I turned back around and looked at Mr. Crabtree. His face looked like a big grape.

"Call an ambulance!" the policeman shouted to Mrs. Cuttahee. Then he ran behind the desk and laid Mr. Crabtree on the floor.

I decided I wasn't needed anymore, so I slunk out the door. Mrs. Cuttahee didn't see me because she was screaming directions into the telephone.

I didn't look back until I had reached the door of his office. Just as I went out, Mrs. Cuttahee was hanging up the phone. I remembered that I had promised Jonathan I'd report to him what had happened. I turned around and raced toward my locker before Mrs. Cuttahee could ask me any questions.

When I opened it, Jonathan was at the back.

"Well?" he said.

"I think I killed him."

"What?"

"I think I killed Mr. Crabtree."

"Why would you do that?"

"All I did was tell him what I needed to do to re-bury you and I think it gave him a heart attack."

"This doesn't sound good."

"I can't help you, Jonathan. I can't do anything about this. You're just going to have to accept the fact that I can't rebury you."

"I refuse to accept that."

"That's not my problem. I can't do anything about this!" I closed the locker door before he could say anything else.

I was halfway across the school grounds before the ambulance pulled to a screeching halt in front of the building.

I needed to talk to Kim.

After thirty-five minutes, I finally found her house and rang the bell. She answered the door. She had a cookie in her mouth. "Want one?"

"No. I couldn't swallow anything right now. I need to talk to you."

"Come on in."

"No. You come out here. I think I killed Mr. Crabtree, and I don't want to be trapped in case I have to leave in a hurry."

She gave me a puzzled look, but came out-side. "What?!"

I told her what happened.

"I have an idea. I need to make a telephone call."

"I'll wait here."

Kim was back in a few minutes. "Everything must be all right. There's no Crabtree at the funeral home. There's no Crabtree in the emergency room at the hospital. I think you're safe."

I did feel a little better, but I was still shaking. "What'd you do?"

I told her.

"Yeah, I can see how he'd be upset, but I told you it wouldn't work. You'll just have to tell Jonathan that he may have to wait fifty more years."

"He'll never accept it, Kim," I said. "He's really serious about this."

Actually, I didn't realize how serious until the next morning.

When I got to school, there was a crowd of kids looking at something that had been painted in big red letters all the way down the hall. When I got closer, I read: DUNNING HEALY WAS HERE.

"Well?"

I turned. Mr. Crabtree was standing behind me, hands on hips, and he looked very much alive.

"Do you have an explanation for this?"

"Yes, sir," I said.

"Well, let me hear it, then!" he snarled.

"The dead kid did it!" I said.

7

Unfortunately, that wasn't the only thing that Jonathan had done.

Mr. Crabtree grabbed me by the elbow and took me on a tour of the school.

Outside the girl's restroom, there was another sign: DUNNING HEALY LOVES JESSICA WIPPLE.

Oh, great! I thought. Jessica Wipple was the one who had seen me talking to my locker. There's no telling what she'd do now. It didn't take me long to find out, though. When we turned the corner on the way to see what else the dead kid had done that Mr. Crabtree thought I had done, I almost ran smack into Jessica Wipple.

I just looked at her, waiting for her to lash out at me, but she smiled and acted kind of shy. "Hi, Dunning," she managed. Then her eyes turned kind of strange and she let out a sigh and walked away.

64

I noticed Mr. Crabtree shaking his head in dismay.

We had now arrived at the main office. Mr. Crabtree opened the door. "Inside," he said.

Mrs. Cuttahee looked up at me and shook her head, too.

Mr. Crabtree pulled me inside his private office. There, on one of the walls, in big red letters, was: DUNNING HEALY SAW MR. CRABTREE AND MS. KIENZLE HOLDING HANDS.

"How did you know this?" he demanded. "We have kept our relationship quiet, because we know the school board policy is strictly against principals dating their teachers, but Ms. Kienzle and I are very fond of each other, and we have had to limit our dates to attending movies and eating in restaurants at least fifty miles away from Belton. I just can't see how it's anybody's business, but we have tried to be discreet, so how did you know?"

"Well, I, uh . . ."

"Her *mother!* That's it. Ms. Kienzle's mother has never liked me. She told you, didn't she?"

Before I could say anything, Mrs. Cuttahee opened the door and said, "Ms. Kienzle needs to talk to you."

Mr. Crabtree looked at me, then said, "I'll talk to you later."

65

When I left the office, Ms. Kienzle looked at me and her face turned bright red.

I didn't know what to say, so I said, "The dead kid did it, Ms. Kienzle."

Her eyes got big and she turned to face the wall.

"Ms. Kienzle, please come into my office," Mr. Crabtree said behind me.

Outside, I thought, if I don't do what Jonathan says, it's just going to get worse.

It occurred to me that, if I could just talk to him calmly, kid to kid, and let him know that doing stuff like writing my name on the wall wasn't going to help matters, he might stop.

I headed toward my locker. When I got there, I opened it and came face to face with Jonathan.

"Well?" Jonathan said.

"Well, what?"

"Did I get my message across?"

"You're trying to blackmail me," I said, "and it's not going to work."

I thought he actually looked a little surprised. "What do you mean?"

"I mean, if you get me kicked out of school, how can I help you?"

He didn't have an answer for that.

"You've asked me to do something impossible.

I told you I mentioned it to Mr. Crabtree, and he thought I was joking."

"Does he think you're joking now?"

"I don't know what he thinks, except that I've been spying on him and Ms. Kienzle. How did you know they were dating?"

"I know everything that goes on in this school, Dunning. There isn't anything that I don't know."

"Blackmail just doesn't work, Jonathan. I think you're going to have to try something else. I just wish you'd keep my name out of it, though. All you're going to do is get me in trouble."

Jonathan looked like he was thinking. I was hoping that I had put a new idea in his head that didn't include me, but would solve my predicament just the same.

"I've got it," Jonathan finally said.

"What?"

He grinned, showing me his awful-looking black teeth. "I can't tell you, but I think it might work."

What had I done now? I wondered. I couldn't imagine what Jonathan had in mind. Just then I saw Ms. Kienzle coming down the hall. "I have to go to class," I said hurriedly. I shut my locker door and hurried down the hall ahead of Ms. Kienzle. I tried not to look at her.

During all the classes I had with her the rest

of that day, she never once looked at me. She stammered and stuttered and finally just gave us work to do at our seats.

Finally, the day was over.

On the way home, I said to Kim, "I'm going to ask Mom and Dad if we can move. I just can't take any more of this."

"Fill me in on everything that happened," Kim said. "You've been vague about it all day."

Actually, I had purposely been vague, because I just wanted it all to go away, but I said, "Mr. Crabtree thinks I'm spying on him and Ms. Kienzle."

"Crabtree and Kienzle? You're kidding."

"No, I'm not. I wish I were."

"Why would he think that?"

"It's Jonathan. He knows everything that goes on at the school. He knows that Mr. Crabtree is dating Ms. Kienzle. Evidently it's against school board policy."

"Oh, this really is news! What else?"

"Nothing else about that. I talked to Jonathan and told him that if he didn't stop writing my name all over school he was going to get me expelled and then he wouldn't have anyone to help him."

"What'd he say?"

"He said he had another idea."

"Did he tell you what it was?"

"No."

"That's scary."

"You're telling me," I said.

I didn't eat or sleep well, because I kept wondering what Jonathan had in mind. He had promised me that he'd quit writing my name on the walls at school, but what he had in mind might be worse.

I tossed and turned all night and finally got up at seven o'clock. I sat on the edge of the bed until Mom came in to wake me up.

"Are you all right?"

"Yes," I said groggily. "I'm just excited about school, that's all." That usually made my parents not want to ask any more questions.

"Oh, I am so thrilled, Dunning. Your father and I like it here, so we were both hoping that you were adjusting. We don't want to move."

So much for asking them if we could move! I thought. "That's nice to hear."

"Well, breakfast is almost ready, so get dressed and come on down."

I started to tell her that I wasn't hungry, but that would just delay her leaving, so I nodded, thinking that maybe I could fake it by moving my food around on the plate some.

It worked. Actually, I was amazed. When I looked down at my plate, it really did look like I had eaten some of it, even though all I had done was rearrange it.

"I just can't eat any more," I said.

Dad looked at my plate. "You've done a pretty good job. There really was a lot." He looked at Mom. "You might give us just a little less in the morning."

"It's hard to judge," she said.

I got up, excused myself, and went up to my bathroom to brush my teeth.

Kim called just as I was leaving. "I think there's going to be trouble."

I felt a knot forming in my stomach. "Trouble? What do you mean?"

"My room's at the back of our house, as you know, but what you probably didn't know is that from my window you can see the cemetery."

"No. I didn't know that."

"Something woke me up in the middle of the night, so I got up and looked out the window." She stopped. "I'm not making this up, Dunning, believe me."

"Hurry up and tell me, Kim. I can take it."

"I saw all of these . . . *dead* kids walking out of the cemetery."

When I didn't say anything, she said, "Are you still there?"

"Yes. Is this a joke?"

"No, Dunning, it isn't. I have better things to do than call you up the first thing in the morning and try to play a practical joke on you."

"How many were there?" I said, lowering my voice so I wouldn't be overheard.

"I counted about twenty."

"Twenty. You mean there were *twenty* dead kids walking out of the cemetery last night?"

"Yes."

"How did you know they were dead kids? Maybe they were just some of the local kids playing pranks."

"I saw their bones, Dunning. They all looked like Jonathan."

I felt myself beginning to hyperventilate. "This doesn't look good. Jonathan told me that he had another idea to try to convince Mr. Crabtree to let us dig up Mrs. Gillingham's fifth grade classroom, so we could rebury him, but it never occurred to me that it would involve other dead kids."

"I wonder what they're planning to do."

"I don't even want to think about it."

Just then the grandfather clock in the living room chimed eight o'clock.

"Oh, great! We're going to be late! Listen, I'll

71

see you at school!" I hung up before Kim could say anything. I grabbed my books and ran out the front door.

I made it to the front door of the school in five minutes.

Just as I opened the door, though, I saw Mrs. Connors running down the hall, screaming, "I taught these kids! They're dead! I taught these kids! They're dead!"

Two dead kids were chasing her.

Kim came up behind me. "What's going on?"

"Some of those dead kids you saw last night are here at the school," I replied.

"Oh, no!"

"Come on. I'm going to my locker!"

Kim and I ran down the hall, turned a corner, and reached my locker in record time. I pulled open the door and came face to face with a new dead kid. "Where's Jonathan?" I demanded.

"He's busy."

"Doing what?"

"What you should have been doing for him. He's trying to convince Mr. Crabtree to rebury him."

"I need to talk to him. This isn't going to work."

"Oh, yes, it will. When we get through, he'll believe us! We all used to go to school here before we died, so we know how it works. We haven't forgotten how to get things done!"

Just then another face appeared at the back of my locker. "Who is it, Bobbie?" a dead girl asked.

"It's that Dunning Healy, the kid who wouldn't help rebury Jonathan."

"Oh, him. Well, shame on you! I mean, we were all resting comfortably in the cemetery, minding our own business, playing cards from time to time in each other's caskets, as dead people usually do, when Jonathan comes and says he's been trying for fifty years to get somebody to rebury him, so he can be with his family. Well, we didn't know his family, because I only died fifteen years ago, but I know how important family can be when you're dead."

"Look, it wasn't that I . . ." I started to say, but then another one of the teachers started running down the hall, screaming, "She used to be in my class, but she died, and now she's back, sitting in her old seat!"

I closed my locker door. "Come on, Kim!"

We started running down the hall.

"Who's that teacher?"

"That was Mrs. Hyatt," Kim said. "Her class is just around the corner."

We rounded the corner and ran into the classroom. All the kids were standing at the back of the room. There was only one student sitting, and it was a dead girl.

"What's happening?" a couple of the students asked. "Who is that?"

"This was my classroom when I died. I didn't get to finish the fourth grade, so I'm going to do it now," the dead girl said. "You might as well sit down, because I'm not leaving!"

"What do you think about my plan?"

Kim and I turned. We were face to face with Jonathan. "Up to this point, not much," I said, "but how did you do it?"

"I simply visited the new cemetery and talked to all the dead kids who never got to finish elementary school over the past fifty years. When I told them that they could finish, they were very excited."

"What?"

"That's right. We're all going to go to school here." He stopped. "Actually, I may have opened up a can of worms, if you'll excuse that expression, because I was only going to do it to force Mr. Crabtree to rebury me, but some of the kids were so excited about coming back to school, that they may not want to leave. In fact, some of them have been talking about going on through junior high, high school, and even college. I mean, after all, what else is there to do in a cemetery except play cards? They have a lot of time on their hands."

"This is awful!" I said.

74

I had no idea how awful it really would be, though.

Kim had evidently miscounted. There were altogether twenty-five new kids in our school who were dead. Two of them were in Ms. Kienzle's room, so two new desks had to be brought in. One dead kid sat next to me.

Mr. Crabtree pleaded and pleaded with them all to go back to the cemetery and do whatever it was that they do, but none of them wanted to.

"I'll rebury Jonathan!" he finally said. "I'll dig up Mrs. Gillingham's fifth grade classroom floor and rebury him in the new cemetery!"

But the School Board wouldn't let him.

"We will not be blackmailed by dead kids!" declared Janie Johnson, president of the School Board. "You'll just have to mainstream those dead kids, Crabtree. Who knows? The other kids can probably learn some things from associating with them!"

Not that it made any difference, anyway. All the dead kids wanted to stay in school. They didn't want to go back to the cemetery. I couldn't believe it. Most of us live kids would have done anything to get out of school, but here were these dead kids who didn't want to leave.

Even when the last bell of the day rang, the dead kids just sat in their seats, begging for more schoolwork.

It was weird.

We live kids were really upset about it, too, because when the dead kids got more work, we got more work.

In fact, the whole town was upset.

"We ought to talk to their parents," the mayor declared at a city council meeting, but no one attending knew how they could go about contacting the dead kids' parents, and the dead kids, who were also attending the meetings, wouldn't say. They just sat there, smiling, and talking about how much fun they were having in school and how it had really changed since they died.

Finally, the furor died down, because the dead kids actually weren't creating any problems, except for, well, the way they looked! Most of them were just skeletons, although some of them still

76

had some of their hair and were wearing the clothes they had been buried in. Mostly they stuck to themselves, but from time to time, they'd be right behind you when you went to your locker or when you thought you were walking down a hallway by yourself.

One morning, Kim pulled me aside before class. "The live kids are starting to blame you."

"*Me?* For what?"

"They think it's all your fault that we have dead kids attending our school. We're the laughingstock of Belton and of all the surrounding towns."

"How's it my fault?"

"It was your locker that Jonathan was living behind. They just don't think you handled the situation very well."

"Well, excuse me, but what else was I supposed to do?"

Kim shrugged. "I didn't say that *I* thought this was your fault. I just said that all of a sudden the other kids are starting to blame you."

"Why all of a sudden?"

"Well, if you want my opinion, I think it's because Rebecca Davidson didn't get on the sixth grade cheerleading squad."

"What happened?"

"Cynthia Morris beat her out."

77

"You mean the Cynthia Morris who's dead?"

"That's the one."

"There's a *dead* girl on the cheerleading squad?

Kim nodded. "Our first football game is Saturday, too."

"Oh, this is just wonderful."

And that was what started it all.

Up until that time, the live kids had started to accept the dead kids, but now the dead kids seemed to be taking over everything. They obviously didn't know their place.

"Tony Barnes wants to be president of the sixth grade?" I cried. "He's dead!"

"Very," Kim said.

"You can't have a dead kid who's president of the sixth grade class. It just isn't . . . *natural!*"

That afternoon, I saw a crowd of sixth grade students at the end of the hall. They were huddled together tightly and talking heatedly about something. I walked over to them.

"What do you want?" Ben McBain demanded.

I shrugged. "I thought I might be interested in what was going on."

"We don't need you around to create more problems for us," Nancy Higgins said.

"What are you talking about?" I said.

"One of the dead kids asked me to go to the

movies with him," Faye MacLeod said. "He said he could get in free." She shuddered.

"Another one of the dead kids asked me to come to his *death*day party," Bill Muller said. "He was going to have it in his casket in the cemetery."

"It's just getting to be too weird at this school," Sara Hess said. "I don't want to come anymore."

Everyone agreed they felt the same way.

"Something's got to be done," Linda McCrumb said. "The dead kids are taking over the school."

"They're also not as nice as they used to be," Ben said. "When they first came here they weren't so bad. Now . . ."

"One dead kid told me if I didn't give him my bookbag, he'd move in with me," Sara said.

Everyone shuddered at that and then looked at me.

"What?"

"What are we going to do?" Linda said. "It can't go on like this."

We all decided we could think better if we went to The Hangout, a hamburger place two blocks from the school.

But when we got there, all of the tables were occupied by dead kids. They were just sitting there, talking to each other. Mr. Kellen, the owner of The Hangout, was just standing around with a stunned look on his face.

I spotted Jonathan in one of the booths at the back and walked over to him. "I thought you guys had gone back to the cemetery."

He looked upset. "I need to talk to you," he whispered. "This is getting out of hand."

"You're telling me," I whispered back.

"I never planned for this to happen, Dunning. I didn't want to go to school. All I ever wanted was to be reburied so I could be with my family and play cards in my casket."

"Something does have to be done, Jonathan. The live kids are getting a little upset at how bold the dead kids are beginning to act. They're taking over the school."

"Can you meet me somewhere tonight? I've been thinking. I may have a plan."

I looked around to see what the kids who were alive were doing. They were giving me dirty looks.

"Name it."

"I'll be at the football field on the south bleachers at midnight."

"Can you make it earlier than that?"

Jonathan shook his head. "I don't think I can get away from the rest of the dead kids before

80

that. They keep wanting to stay out later and later."

"I'll be there."

I stood up and walked back over to the live kids.

"Well?" Ben said.

"I'm going to meet Jonathan tonight at midnight at . . ." I stopped. I suddenly decided that it might be better not to name the place. Tension was high between the dead kids and the live kids, and I didn't want anything to happen to this meeting. "We'll get everything settled then. Jonathan thinks he may have a way to get the dead kids back to the cemetery for good."

That seemed to help, although several of the live kids were still irritated that there weren't any empty booths at The Hangout.

I had to be in bed by ten, so I set my alarm for eleven-thirty. I knew I'd never wake up if I didn't.

When the alarm went off, it sounded like a church bell ringing in my ear, and I just knew that Mom and Dad had probably heard it, too.

I got out of bed and went to my door and listened, but there were no other sounds in the house.

I turned on my bedside lamp and dressed hurriedly.

81

I got my house key and then tiptoed down the stairs and out the front door.

There was a moon, so I didn't need a flashlight, but I had taken one, anyway, because I thought there might be some dark corners on my way to the football field.

Two blocks from my house, I had to hide behind a bush while a couple of dead kids passed. I couldn't believe they were still out, wandering the streets, but then Jonathan had said that they didn't like to go back to the cemetery until midnight.

Finally, the dead kids had passed, and I crossed the street.

It took me five more blocks before I got to the football field. The gate was locked, but I was able to climb the metal fence that surrounded it. While I was doing it, I was wondering how Jonathan was going to get in.

This had sure changed my opinion of what dead people could do. The dead kids didn't go through walls or anything like that. They had to go in and out of doors just like the rest of us. The only thing that they did differently was to go back to the cemetery every night and sleep in their caskets until it was time to go to school.

I had also wondered how they got out of their caskets, but Jonathan had said that *all* cemeteries were like underground cities, with tunnels from one casket to another, so that the dead people could open up the trapdoors in the bottoms of their caskets and go visit the other dead people in the cemetery. I reminded him that the cemetery under the school was just one big cavern, and he said that it had all been eroded by time and neglect.

Of course, in order to leave the cemetery, the dead kids had come out of one of those sunken places you see around old graves. Jonathan said that it's like a tunnel up to the ground and that the dead people simply lift up the ground like a lid, come out, do what they have to, and then go back to the cemetery the same way. To the untrained eye, Jonathan said, the lid to the underground cemetery city looks just like another piece of earth, except that it may be a bit sunken.

I finally found the bleachers where Jonathan said he was going to meet me.

I sat down and waited.

For some reason, there seemed to be all kinds of strange sounds. I even thought that in the distance I had heard laughing. I looked at my watch. The glowing hand and numerals told me that it was now a quarter past midnight.

"Where are you, Jonathan?" I muttered.

"Jonathan won't be coming," a voice behind me said.

I whipped around, almost taking my head off at the same time. I was looking at a dead adult! "Who are you?"

"It doesn't matter who I am. You just need to go on home and forget that you had a meeting with Jonathan. He's not coming."

"Where is he?"

"He's somewhere where he can't destroy our plans."

"What plans?"

The dead man smiled. "Well, what can it hurt to tell you? We've already decided to do it, so nothing can stop us now."

I shivered. I wasn't quite sure I wanted to hear all of this.

"We were all quite content in the cemetery. After all, some of us have been there for a long time, and we have learned to live with it." He laughed at his joke. "Get it? *Live* with it?"

"I get it, but I don't think it's very funny."

He shrugged. "Oh, well, we dead people have a different sense of humor than you live people."

"Just tell me what you were going to say."

"Well, as I was saying, we dead people were perfectly content with our lives, living peaceably in our caskets, playing cards, visiting with each

84

other from time to time, and talking about how we had died, but after our kids started going to school and talking about how much fun they were having, we adults decided that maybe we weren't having such a great time after all, so we had a meeting tonight to talk about it."

"What did you decide to do?"

"We decided that we were all going to go back to our old jobs."

"How can you do that?" I asked. "What will the live people do without them?"

The dead man shrugged. "They'll just have to learn to get along, that's all. Why should they be the only ones working? We dead people have rights, too."

This was getting to be too much. "I don't think this is going to work," I said. "Jonathan and I were planning to talk about how to get the dead kids to stay in the cemetery."

"Well, Jonathan won't be talking about that anymore. Jonathan isn't part of our plan."

I stood up. "There isn't going to be any plan, mister!" I shouted. "No dead man is going to take over my dad's job!"

I started to jump off the bleachers, but the dead man grabbed my arm. "We will not be denied our rights. I have just as much right to your dad's job as he does. After all, it was mine before I died, and I plan to take it back!"

I couldn't believe it. This dead man was Mr. Hooper! I jerked loose. "Over my dead body!" I shouted and wished I hadn't used those words.

I started running out onto the middle of the field.

Mr. Hooper started running after me, but skeleton people can't run very fast, I had discovered, so I was able to stay ahead of him.

I finally reached the opposite fence, and I began scaling it, but Mr. Hooper was faster than I had thought he would be, and he grabbed at my ankle just as I jumped over and landed on the other side.

"You won't be able to stop us!" Mr. Hooper cried.

"We'll never stop trying!" I shouted.

I didn't look back. I had to get home to warn Dad, so he could warn the rest of the people in Belton. I also had to find Jonathan. If a dead person's life could be in danger, I was sure his was!

I ran all the way home.

But I was astonished at how quickly Mr. Hooper was able to climb over the metal fence and start chasing me. I never knew skeletons could do that!

When I got to my front door, Mr. Hooper was at the corner, under the street lamp, running as fast as his skeleton legs would carry him, but I got the door unlocked and was inside just as Mr. Hooper ran up our front walk.

I leaned against the door, panting for breath, not knowing what to expect, but after a couple of minutes, when Mr. Hooper hadn't tried to beat the door down, I thought I was safe, but I wasn't going to open the door to check.

Just as I turned away to head up to my room, I heard talking on the other side of the door.

I put my ear to it. I could just make out what

the dead man was saying. "Tell your father that I want my old job back, Dunning."

"No way," I muttered and started for the stairs. I had no idea how long Mr. Hooper would stay outside, but I was going up to my room to go to bed. I just didn't want to deal with this anymore today.

But outside my parents' bedroom, I stopped. I couldn't just forget about it. I knew something that affected everybody in Belton. The sooner somebody did something about it, the better off we'd all be.

I knocked on the door.

There was no answer.

I opened it slowly and peeked in.

By the night-light, I could see Mom and Dad sleeping. I crept over and shook Dad's shoulder.

He came awake with a "Whoa! Who's doing that?" and awakened Mom.

"Dunning, what in the world's wrong?" Mom cried. "Did you have a bad dream? Do you need some water?"

Honestly! Mom still thinks I'm a baby. "No, I just need to talk to Dad, Mom."

Dad looked at the clock on his bedside table. "Dunning, it's almost two o'clock in the morning. What in the world . . ." He rubbed his eyes. "Why are you dressed?" He looked back at his clock.

"Did this thing stop? Did the electricity go off? Oh, my gosh! I'm late for work. Is that it?"

"No, Dad, no! It's nothing like that, but I do need to talk to you. Can we go downstairs so we won't disturb Mom?"

Mom had already lain back down. Thank goodness she needs her sleep, because I didn't want to deal with how she'd react to all of this.

Dad got out of bed and put on his robe and slippers. He followed me downstairs.

When we got to the kitchen, I poured myself a glass of milk. Dad wanted one, too, so I poured another one.

Dad took a sip of his milk and then said, "Okay, Dunning, what's going on?"

"Well, you know the dead kids who are going to school with us?"

Dad shook his head. "It's weird, but they have rights, too, as far as we can tell."

"Well, now the dead *adults* are talking about their rights, too."

Dad looked puzzled. "What do you mean?"

"I ran into Mr. Hooper tonight."

"Mr. Hooper?"

"The Mr. Hooper who had your job before you did."

Dad's eyes went wide. "He's dead, Dunning. That's how I got the job."

"I know he's dead, Dad, but so are all those kids in our school, and that doesn't seem to make much difference to the School Board."

"Well, uh, what'd he want?"

"Well, I was supposed to meet Jonathan, so we could plan a way to get the dead kids to stay in the cemetery, but Mr. Hooper showed up instead. He and the other dead adults have done something with Jonathan."

"Why?"

"The dead adults have seen how happy the dead kids are, now that they're in school and doing something besides playing cards in their caskets, so all of the dead adults have decided they want to do something else, too. That won't happen if Jonathan convinces the dead kids to go back to the cemetery." I looked at Dad. "The dead adults want their old jobs back."

"They can't have their old jobs back, Dunning. They're *dead!*"

"They don't care, Dad."

"Well, I care! We moved here from Detroit so I could take this job. I am not going to give it up to the person whose death enabled me to get it in the first place!" He sat down at the kitchen table and took another drink of milk.

"Mr. Hooper followed me home, too. In fact, he may still be on the front porch."

Dad turned pale. "You mean there's a dead person sitting on our front porch right now?"

"Unless he's already gone back to the cemetery."

Dad stood up. "Well, we'll just see about this." He stormed out of the kitchen and headed for the front door.

"Dad! I don't know if that's a good idea or not. He chased me all the way home. If he gets in our house, there's no telling what he'll do."

Dad stopped just before he reached the front door. "Maybe you're right." He thought for a minute. "I'd better call George Formichael. He's the only city councilman I can really deal with." He looked up at me. "You go on to bed. There's nothing you can do now."

"I'm sorry for all of this mess, Dad."

"It's not your fault, Dunning."

"Well, all the kids think it is. After all, Jonathan was behind *my* locker, and if I could have figured out a way to rebury him, none of this would have happened."

Dad didn't say anything. He was probably thinking that maybe I was to blame for all of this after all.

When I awakened the next morning, I sensed that there was something really wrong. I got up

91

and looked out my window. There were dead people everywhere!

Across the street, I could see a dead man and a dead woman standing on Mrs. Logan's front porch. They seemed to be arguing with her. What in the world was going on? I wondered.

I hurriedly dressed and went downstairs.

I found Mom in her robe, leaning up against the front door. My first thought was that Mr. Hooper was still outside and that he had said something to upset her.

"Mom?"

Mom turned. She had the strangest expression on her face.

"What's wrong, Mom?"

"The doorbell rang, so I went to answer the door, and standing there, right on our front porch, was a dead man and a dead woman demanding that we move out of their house."

"What?"

"That's what I said. 'What?' They said they were living here when they died and that we have no right to be here, since they've decided to come back. What were they talking about, Dunning?"

I reminded her about the dead kids at school.

"Well, I know about that, but there wasn't anything that could be done. Those kids were going

92

to school when they died, so it only seemed fitting that they be allowed to finish their education."

"The dead adults feel the same way, Mom. They're tired of just playing cards in their caskets and visiting with other dead people. They want to get on with their lives."

"How can they get on with their lives, Dunning, if they're dead?"

"That's what we're all wondering, too, Mom."

Then I thought the only right thing to do was fill her in on what had happened at the football field last night, how Mr. Hooper had chased me home, how he had said he wanted his job back, and how Dad had probably stayed up all night to sort things out.

"Where is Dad, anyway?"

"He left me a note saying that there was an emergency city council meeting this morning at seven o'clock."

I looked at my watch. It was seven-thirty. "I need to eat breakfast and then go to school, because I have a feeling this is going to be a very interesting day."

I wolfed down a bowl of cereal, brushed my teeth, then grabbed my book bag and headed out the door.

If anything, there were even more dead adults on the streets now. It also seemed that every other house I passed had a dead man and a dead woman on the porch arguing with the live owner about who should be living in the house.

When I got to school, all of the dead kids were playing on the playground equipment. I had hoped that maybe Jonathan would be among them, but he wasn't, so Mr. Hooper had probably been serious when he said that he had taken care of Jonathan, so he couldn't scuttle the adults' plans to start living in Belton again.

I saw a crowd of live kids huddled together on the steps of the school building. I didn't really want to deal with them this early, but before I could slip around and go in the back door, Bill Muller saw me and they all came running over.

"Okay, what gives?" Bill demanded. "I thought you and Jonathan were going to solve this problem."

"Yeah!" everyone else shouted.

"The dead kids are still here," Linda said. "I thought they'd be gone."

"Yeah!" everyone else repeated.

I looked over at the dead kids. They were ignoring us, they were having so much fun sliding down the slide and riding the merry-go-round.

"There's a hitch."

"A *hitch?*" Faye said. "You mean, like you didn't do anything?"

I took a deep breath and told them what had happened at the football field. "They've done something with Jonathan so he can't talk the other dead kids into going back to the cemetery."

Everyone just looked at me.

"It gets worse. Now the dead adults want to come back and take over their old jobs and move back into their old houses."

"This is crazy! This can't be happening!" Sara said. "I feel like I'm in the middle of some horror movie!"

"Yeah," I said. "Unfortunately, I yelled 'cut!' last night and nothing happened!"

We were saved by the bell.

All of us live kids started into the school building, but the dead kids just stayed where they were.

Mr. Crabtree finally had to blow a whistle. Reluctantly they stopped playing and started toward the front of the building.

We all hurried to our classrooms, so we'd be seated when they got there. The dead kids had decided that they could sit wherever they wanted to, so if you weren't already in your seat, they'd take it.

Not much got done that day.

All the dead kids wanted to talk about was how their parents had come back to take over their

95

old jobs. Since some of the dead adults had been teachers, Ms. Kienzle and Mr. Jones were very concerned.

Around ten o'clock, the dead teachers started coming into the classrooms, demanding to have their classes back.

"Can you imagine having a dead person for a teacher?" Kim whispered to me.

I didn't say it, but I was thinking that sometimes Mr. Jones's lectures were so boring that I thought he was already dead himself. I probably wouldn't notice any difference.

During lunch, Kim and I saw Mr. Crabtree arguing with a dead man.

"He must have been a principal when he was alive," Kim said.

"This can't go on," I said. "We have to find Jonathan. I just know he could figure this out. After all, he's dead. He understands dead people."

"Where could he be, though?" Kim said.

I thought for a minute. Then it hit me. "What's the most obvious place?"

Kim shook her head. "I don't know."

"His casket!"

"Why? I mean, if he were in his casket, he'd just come out to see what's going on. That's where he always slept."

"Yeah, but if they did something to it, like locking it somehow, then he couldn't get out."

"Are you sure?"

"Yes. Dead people can't work magic. They're not exactly like live people, but they still have to do some things the way we do."

"You may be right."

"We need to check it out, anyway. We don't have any other leads."

We finished our lunches and hurried back to our classroom.

"I'd give anything if we could go out for recess again."

"You know what happens if we're not in our classroom when the dead kids come in. They take our seats and they use our stuff."

I could hardly concentrate for the rest of the afternoon, but we didn't do much anyway. Ms. Kienzle and Mr. Jones had obviously decided that it would be simpler to share their teaching duties with the two dead teachers who were demanding their classes back, so most of the time was spent in their explaining to the dead teachers what we were doing and catching them up on the last fifty years of what had happened in the United States while they had been buried.

Finally, the bell rang.

Kim and I stayed seated, pretending to finish

97

up an assignment. Then, when everyone was gone, we got up and left the classroom.

I was glad that nobody else was in the hallway where my locker was.

When we got to it, I opened the door. I had hoped to see Jonathan's skeleton face, but all I saw was the back of the locker, so I pushed against it and it opened.

Then Kim and I climbed into the locker and started crawling through the tunnel that led to the old cemetery under the school. I was just glad she had remembered to bring her flashlight.

Finally, we reached the large open area, and Kim shined her flashlight toward where Jonathan's casket was supposed to be.

"It's not there!" I cried. "They've moved it!"

"There it is!" Kim had moved the flashlight over so that it lit up the opposite side of his cemetery.

We ran toward it.

When we got there, some metal object reflected the light from the flashlight.

"I thought so," I said. "They've put a padlock on it so Jonathan can't get out."

"He'll suffocate!" Kim cried.

"He can't suffocate," I said. "He's dead. The only thing that will happen is that he won't be able to get out."

We looked at the lock. "It's a combination," I said. "There's no way we'll figure it out."

"Two to the left, three to the right, four . . ."

"Jonathan!" I cried. "Can you hear me?"

"Certainly I can hear you. Now just open this casket so I can get out!"

Jonathan knew the entire combination because it was his old lock. We had him out in just a couple of minutes.

I told him everything that had happened.

"That figures," he said, "but I've got another plan."

"I've got a plan, too, but we've got to get you out of here first," I said.

"I can't leave without my casket, so where can I go?" Jonathan asked. "I don't like sleeping on the ground."

"You can stay with me," I said. I couldn't believe that I was asking a dead kid to spend the night with me, but I didn't have any choice. Jonathan was absolutely essential to my plan, and I couldn't take a chance on anything happening to him.

Suddenly, we heard voices coming from the area of the tunnel.

"Someone's coming," Kim whispered. "What are we going to do?"

I felt myself go all cold inside. I looked at Jonathan. "Is there another way out?"

He hesitated for just a second.

"If there is, Jonathan, you need to tell us. If they find us in here, they'll probably put all three of us inside your casket, and Kim and I'll never get out alive."

"Yes, there's another way out. It's just that only dead people are supposed to know about it. But I guess the rules of the game have changed. Follow me."

We ran with Jonathan to the far edge of the cemetery. He pulled away a large tangle of roots and exposed what was sort of like a narrow underground lane. As soon as the three of us were in the lane, Jonathan replaced the tangle of roots. "The dead people who used to live in this cemetery had started building this lane to connect the old cemetery with the new cemetery that was going to be built across the street, but before they completed it, the people in the town decided to put the new cemetery on the other side of town and move the residents of the old cemetery to it."

The underground lane suddenly opened into another, smaller underground room.

"They had only buried a few people here when they decided to move everyone, so that's why it's not as large as where we were."

Behind us we heard shouts.

"They've discovered I'm gone!" Jonathan whispered.

"We'd better get out of here, then," I said.

"I agree," Kim said.

"I don't think they'll find us. They may not even remember that they dug this, but maybe we'd better not take any chances."

Jonathan didn't need any light, but Kim shined her flashlight so that she and I could see.

On the other side of the small room, Jonathan said, "This way!" He grabbed a root and started climbing.

"Where does this lead, Jonathan?" I called to him.

"It goes up inside a dead tree trunk, and we come out in that clump of big trees on the other side of the school."

I remembered seeing them before.

Jonathan was now halfway up the trunk and reached down to give Kim a boost up. I could tell she didn't want to grab hold of his skeleton hand, but there wasn't any other way around it. Besides, I didn't want her offending Jonathan. "Take it," I whispered.

She grimaced but grabbed hold of his hand, and Jonathan pulled her up into the hollow trunk of the big tree.

I followed.

There were several knots we could look out of to see if anyone was watching us, but there was no one around, so slowly the three of us crawled out.

"We should take the long way home," I said. "They're probably still looking for us."

But since I didn't really know a long way home, Kim agreed to show us. We headed away from the school building. Two blocks away, we went down the steep embankment of Belton Creek and followed the heavily foliaged banks for what seemed like forever. Several times we had to hide behind trees and under bridges to keep from being seen by dead people who seemed to be everywhere.

Finally, Kim said, "We climb back up here and we're two blocks from your house, Dunning."

I was glad, because I was exhausted.

I looked at my watch. Dad wouldn't be home. I didn't know about Mom. I could only hope that she was out doing errands.

When we reached the top of the embankment, Kim stopped and said, "There are some dead people coming. Get back."

We waited until they had passed.

Then we dashed across the street and into the alley behind our house.

"I'll leave you here," Kim said. "Good luck!"

"Thanks," I said. I'm sure she was referring to

the luck I'd need in explaining why I had invited a dead kid to spend the night with me.

Jonathan and I went through our back gate, up the walk, and onto the back porch.

The back door was locked, so I got the key out of the hanging flower pot and opened it.

"Mom?" I called.

Usually, if Mom's home, the back door is unlocked, because she's always working in the flowers, but I didn't want to take a chance.

"Mom?" I called again.

I finally decided that we were alone, so I took Jonathan up to my room.

"No one will find you. Mom and Dad never come up here, unless it's to get something out of the attic, and even then they never really come into my room. They think this is my private domain and that they shouldn't come in unless they're invited."

"Boy, things have certainly changed since I was a kid fifty years ago," Jonathan said. "Father ruled the house, and my mother, my sister, and I did exactly as we were told."

"We've studied about that in history class," I said. "Well, are you hungry?"

Jonathan just looked at me. "Dead people don't eat anymore."

"Oh, yeah. I forgot." I felt really dumb.

"It was strange at first, because every time I would see food that I had liked to eat when I was alive, I'd start to take some, but then I'd remember that I didn't eat anymore."

"It must really be strange to be dead."

Jonathan nodded his skull. "Yes, it does take some getting used to."

"Well, I'm hungry, so if you don't mind, I'll run downstairs and get some cookies and milk, and then we'll figure out what we're going to do to solve this."

I went downstairs and hurriedly poured myself a glass of milk and grabbed a handful of store-bought cookies. I was suddenly hungry for some of Kim's dad's cookies, but I didn't think it was the time to go over there and ask her for some.

Just then, I heard the front door opening.

Could it be some of the dead people? I wondered.

I peeked around the kitchen door and glimpsed Mom coming in.

"Oh, hi, Mom!" I called to her. "I just came down to get some milk and cookies. I need to get back upstairs."

"I just had the most awful experience, Dunning. I was in this dress shop, and I couldn't get waited on, because this dead woman was arguing with the salesclerk about who should be helping me. It seems this dead woman used to work there and wanted her old job back. Well, I absolutely didn't want this dead woman bringing me dresses to try on. It was positively ghoulish. Something has to be done about this." She shivered.

"Well, I need to get back upstairs. I have a lot of work to do." If Mom knew that there was a dead kid in our house right now and that he planned to spend the night with me, there's no telling what she'd do.

I found Jonathan propped up on my bed. All of a sudden I realized that he'd probably be sleeping with me, too. I mean, when you invite a friend over to spend the night, he has to sleep somewhere, doesn't he, and I didn't think I could ask Jonathan to sleep on the floor. Of course, I wouldn't have minded doing that myself, but then I was afraid that Jonathan would be offended and reconsider helping me to solve this problem. Oh, well, it would just be for one night. Surely I could stand sleeping with a dead person for one night.

"You sure you don't want a cookie?" I said.

Jonathan shook his skull. "You've got a nice room here."

"Thanks. Well, what are we going to do, Jonathan?" I had decided to find out what else he had in mind before I told him my plan. "Things are really going downhill fast. The kids at school are getting upset because the dead kids have taken over, and now the adults are getting upset, because the dead adults are taking over. Something's got to give."

"All I want is to be reburied so I can play cards," Jonathan said.

"How are we going to convince the dead people to go back to the cemetery?"

"I think if we can get the dead kids to go back, the dead adults will go back, too."

"But how can we do that?"

"Hand me a pencil and a piece of paper," Jonathan said.

I got up and got a pencil and a piece of paper and handed them to him.

"I'm going to write down names of four kids, Dunning, along with their addresses, and I want you to bring them here." Jonathan started writing. Then he handed me the list:

1. *Mack James*   *4 East No. 7*
2. *Latham Edwards*   *12 South No. 13*
3. *Kathy Hooper*   *22 North No. 2*
4. *Renee Laging*   *5 West No. 45*

"These are strange addresses, Jonathan. Besides, I don't know my way around Belton very well. I'll never find them."

"They're not in Belton, Dunning; they're in the Belton Cemetery. I want you to go get those kids and bring them here. They're the leaders of the dead kids. I need to find out the mood of the dead kids before we can decide what to do about all of this."

"You want me to go to the cemetery by myself and talk to these dead kids and try to get them to come back to my house?"

Jonathan nodded. "Well, you don't have to go by yourself. You could get Kim to go with you."

That'll be the day, I thought.

Actually, when I telephoned her, she agreed, so I told her I'd meet her in front of her house just before midnight, because that's when Jonathan thought the dead kids would all be back in the cemetery.

I went down to dinner, which I couldn't eat very well, just thinking about what I had to do that night, but Mom and Dad were so preoccupied with trying to solve their dead adult problems, that they didn't pay much attention to me.

"I'm going to go up to my room, take my bath, and get in bed and do my homework."

Even that didn't elicit anything more than an "Okay. We'll see you in the morning."

Toward ten o'clock, I began to get so sleepy that I couldn't hold my eyes open, but I still felt so strange with Jonathan lying next to me that I didn't want to sleep.

I did keep dozing, though, but I'd wake with a start every so often and Jonathan would say, "Go to sleep. I'll wake you up before midnight." I had given him a pack of cards, which he had been playing with since we got to my house.

"Don't dead people ever sleep?"

Jonathan shook his skull. "That's one of the misconceptions that live people have about us. We never sleep. We just play cards all the time when we're in our caskets."

That still sounded so strange to me. It made me wonder what other misconceptions live people had about dead people.

Then, suddenly, I felt this bony hand on my shoulder, shaking me, and I jumped up.

Jonathan was looking at me with a horrible grin on his face. Had this all been a joke? I wondered. What was he planning to do to me?

"It's time to get up," Jonathan said.

I blinked. Then I realized that the horrible grin was just the way he normally looked.

I sat up. My heart was pounding. "Is it time?"

Jonathan nodded his skull.

I stood up and took a deep breath. When would this nightmare end? I wondered.

I went to my bedroom door, opened it, and listened. Mom and Dad had evidently gone to bed already, because there were no sounds coming from downstairs.

I turned back to Jonathan. "I guess I'd better be going," I said.

"Tell all four of them that I need to talk to them. I think they'll come. But Dunning, when you knock on their graves, do it quietly, because most of them live with their parents, and if you awaken their parents, then they might not get to come."

"Okay. I'll be careful." I didn't like the idea that I might have to deal with some dead parents, but I didn't know what else to do.

I grabbed my jacket and left the room.

When I got to the front door, I opened it slowly and peeked out. I was still paranoid about this whole thing being a setup, but nobody was waiting for me outside the front door.

As I started down the street, I didn't see any dead people around anywhere. I guess that they had finally gotten used to being away from the cemetery, so that it wasn't a big deal, and that their hours were a little more normal.

Kim was waiting for me behind the big bush in front of her house. "I thought you weren't coming."

"I really didn't want to," I admitted. "I'd like

nothing more than to be asleep in my bed right now, without a dead person lying next to me."

Kim shivered. "I like Jonathan, but I can't imagine how you could sleep in the same bed with him."

"I didn't want to offend him, Kim. I'm counting on his helping us solve this mess we're in."

All the way to the cemetery, ten blocks away from Kim's house, we stayed away from the streetlights and crossed the streets only after we had made sure no cars were coming.

We didn't see anybody at all.

I guessed the live people simply didn't want to be out after dark anymore, because they were afraid they'd run into some dead people.

Finally, we reached the cemetery.

I pulled the list from my pocket. "Here are the four dead kids Jonathan said we should bring to my house."

Kim looked at the list. "What do these numbers mean?"

"Those will tell us where their graves are," I replied. "Mack James is buried in Section four East, Plot Number seven."

"You mean dead people actually have addresses?"

"Of course. How else will you find them if you come to the cemetery?"

Kim shivered.

In the middle of the cemetery, we found a map, but instead of streets, it had the section and lot numbers, so it was easy to locate where each of the four kids was buried.

"Let's try Mack James first," Kim said. "He's the closest."

Kim shined her flashlight along the path that led to Section 4 East, Plot No. 7, and we finally got there.

I looked at the tombstone. It said THE JAMES FAMILY and gave the dates of death of the four people buried there. Mack was only fourteen when he died twenty-five years ago. "Jonathan said to be quiet, so we wouldn't wake up the parents," I told Kim.

"That sounds like a good idea," Kim said.

"I wonder how we should do this," I said.

Kim shrugged. "I guess we just knock, like you'd do if you were going to their house."

I knelt down on the ground and started knocking on the marble slab that marked Mack's grave. I didn't want to knock too loudly, because I didn't want to wake up his parents. I also didn't want to skin my knuckles.

We waited, but there was no sound from inside the grave.

"Knock again," Kim said.

I knocked again. "Mack!" I whispered as loudly as I dared. "Mack!"

We waited a couple more minutes. "Maybe he's not home," I said.

Suddenly a boy in an old-fashioned-looking suit appeared at the foot of the grave.

I gulped. "Mack?"

The boy nodded. "Yes?"

"How'd you get here?" Kim asked.

"It's a secret that only dead people know," Mack said.

I suddenly remembered the tree trunk at the old cemetery and what Jonathan had told me about secret entrances.

"What do you want?" Mack said. "I was busy playing cards."

"Uh, Jonathan sent us," I said. "He wants to see you and Latham Edwards, Kathy Hooper, and Renee Laging at my house tonight. He wants to ask you something."

"I think I know what it is," Mack said.

I didn't know how he could know if I didn't, but I said, "I'll go get Latham, Kathy, and Renee."

"I'll get them and bring them to your house. Their parents might not let them come if you do it."

I took a deep breath. Thank goodness for that, I thought. "Well, thanks, Mack," I said. "Just

113

come on to my house. We'll be waiting." I grabbed
Kim's arm and started to leave. "Oh, you don't
know my address, do you?"

"Yes, we do," Mack said. "We know where all
the live people live in Belton. But wait for us to
get back. We'll all walk together."

That sent chills down my spine.

I wasn't quite sure this was such a good idea
after all. It had been bad enough just having one
dead person in my house, but now we'd have five,
and we'd be outnumbered if they decided to
take over.

"I'll be right back," Mack said.

Kim and I watched as Mack headed across the cemetery to get Latham, Kathy, and Renee.

"Do you think they'll want to come?" Kim said. "What if they don't? What'll we do then?"

I shrugged. Then I shivered. This whole thing was so crazy. When we moved to Belton, I would never have believed I'd be standing in the cemetery after midnight waiting for a dead kid to get three other dead kids so they could go home with me and we could all have a meeting with another dead kid. I had to be out of my mind.

Above us, a cloud slowly covered the moon until it was so dark that we couldn't see anything.

"Should I turn on my flashlight?" Kim asked.

"I don't know. Maybe we'd better wait a few minutes. Dead kids don't need light. It might make them mad. Let's just wait until we *hear* them coming."

115

We waited for what seemed like a long time but then we heard movement from the other side of the cemetery.

I held my breath. It had suddenly occurred to me that it might be angry dead parents coming to see what we were doing in the cemetery so late.

Then we heard whispering, and I thought I recognized Mack's voice.

"Mack?" I called softly.

"Yes?" came his reply.

I relaxed.

Kim turned on the flashlight, but the cloud that had covered the moon had moved away and we could see well enough that we really didn't need it.

At last, Mack, Latham, Kathy, and Renee were standing in front of us. They didn't seem to be too happy.

"What's this meeting all about?" Renee demanded.

"Jonathan wants to talk to you about the problems you're having," I said.

Latham snorted. "We dead kids aren't having any problems. It's you live kids who have the problems."

I didn't like the anger in his voice. "Well, we just want to get things sorted out," I said hurriedly. "Now that the dead adults are wanting their old jobs back and their old houses back, we've got some bigger problems."

"What's wrong with that?" Kathy demanded.

"Listen, it's cold," I said. "We need to hurry."

"We're not cold," Mack said. "It's because you have blood that you're cold."

"Yeah," Latham said. "If you didn't have blood like us, it wouldn't matter."

"Maybe somebody should take out all of your blood," Kathy said. "Why should you have blood and not us?"

"Let's not talk about that here," I said. "That's what Jonathan wanted us all to talk about."

Kim turned to me. "Jonathan wants to talk about why we have blood and they don't?"

Renee snickered.

I started walking away. This conversation was going downhill, fast. "Come on. If we don't hurry, we'll all be late for school in the morning."

For a few minutes, no one moved, but finally I heard the crunch of their skeleton feet on the gravel walkway.

By the time we reached the gates of the cemetery, Kim was beside me, and the dead kids were behind us.

"Don't you dare go off and leave me with them all by myself in a cemetery at midnight!" she whispered between clenched teeth.

117

It took us about twenty minutes to reach my house. I fumbled with the key for five more, before I finally got the door unlocked. Before I opened it, I said, "We'll need to be as quiet as possible, so we won't wake up my parents."

"Are you embarrassed to have dead kids in your house?" Latham said.

"I lived in this house longer than you have," Kathy said. "You probably have my room."

I looked at her. Kathy Hooper, I thought. Kathy *Hooper!* Mr. Hooper's daughter, who died way before he did. Oh, my gosh! What have I done?

"I think you should make him move out!" Renee said. "You wouldn't have left if you hadn't died."

"I hope you haven't messed it up. I had just redecorated it the day before the accident."

I took a deep breath. It wouldn't do any good to argue about that now. "Here we go," I said.

I slowly opened the door, and the six of us went inside.

"Tacky. Really tacky!" Kathy said. She was looking around the living room. "Someone has really poor taste."

I started to get mad, because I thought we had a pretty living room, but then I thought, She's *dead!* How can you get mad at what a dead person is saying?

They started following me across the living room to the stairs, but by the time we had reached the first step, Kathy was leading. She said, "This way."

"This is my house now, Kathy," I said.

"Not for long," Kathy said, as she started up the stairs. "My parents and I are planning on moving back in and my dad's going to take over his old job from your dad."

Kim grabbed my arm. "She may not want to leave once she gets up to your room."

"I'd thought of that," I whispered back. Of course, it was too late to do anything about that now.

We had finally reached my room.

Jonathan was lying on the bed, watching television. He turned it off when we came in.

"Thanks for coming," he said to the dead kids. He stood up. "Sit down. I need to talk to you."

"Why should we listen to you?" Latham demanded. "You don't even live in the cemetery."

"You're right, but I should be there, and the reason I'm not is that I was hardheaded and didn't follow the rules of cemetery etiquette."

Cemetery etiquette? I thought. What was that?

"What are you talking about?" Kathy said.

119

"There are rules and regulations concerning behavior for living in cemeteries," Jonathan said. "People don't pay a lot of attention to them anymore, but when I died they were still very important. Unfortunately, I ignored them, and look what happened to me. I've been living in an abandoned cemetery for over fifty years, waiting to be reburied."

"You've been dead too long," Latham said. "Nobody pays any attention to cemetery etiquette anymore."

Jonathan looked at me. Was this his plan? I wondered. If it was, it wasn't working. I might have to put my own plan into effect before I was ready to.

"Actually, I'm unhappy," Renee suddenly admitted. "I just wish it was like it used to be, where all we did was stay in our caskets and play cards."

I felt a sudden surge of hope. Maybe all wasn't lost after all.

"Tell me about it," Jonathan said.

Renee sighed. "Well, I thought that going to school would be fun, you know, getting away from the casket and all, but it hasn't turned out to be as much fun as I thought it would. It was fun at first, because we sort of didn't have to obey anybody. Our parents were still all in their caskets

120

visiting and playing cards, not paying any attention to us, but then they decided they wanted to go back to their old jobs and their old houses, so then everything changed."

"What do you mean?" Kim asked.

"Renee's right. It's not fun anymore," Kathy said. "Now our parents are back on live time instead of dead time and they make us come in at a certain time and do our homework and all the things that live kids have to do. I mean, we're not alive, we're dead, so why should we have to act like live kids?"

"We can solve that," Jonathan said.

"How?" Mack said.

"I have a feeling that if you go back to the cemetery for good, your parents will want to go back, too," Jonathan said.

"I don't want to go back," Latham said. "I want to stay! I like swinging and sliding and riding on the merry-go-round." He stood up. "I'm going to go tell my parents where you're hiding, Jonathan. They'll put a stop to this! We dead people are going to take over this town and take back what was ours before we died!"

He ran out of the room.

I looked at everybody. "Oh, this is bad. This is really bad!" I said.

"Maybe not," Jonathan said. "I have another plan."

I was sick of Jonathan's plans. They weren't working. He was an old-fashioned dead person. He didn't have any ideas that would appeal to modern dead people. That was what we needed.

"I have a plan, too," I said hurriedly. It was time to act. "What do you think would make the dead kids want to stay in the cemetery?"

Everyone just looked at me.

"The playground!" I shouted.

"You mean *our* playground?" Kim said. "You're out of your mind!"

I just smiled.

Jonathan was smiling, too. "I think you're right, Dunning. I can't believe I didn't think of that myself."

Mack, Renee, and Kathy were nodding their skulls.

"Oh, I'd love to have a playground in our cemetery. It does get a little boring playing cards all the time," Mack said. "I mean, it's really an adult game. They all enjoy doing it, visiting from casket to casket, but, well, if we have a playground, being dead wouldn't be so boring!"

Kim looked at me. "How are you going to do this?" she demanded. I could tell that she was ticked off at the idea of giving up all of the playground equipment.

"We'll move it piece by piece," I said. I looked

122

at the dead kids. "No offense, but I think the live kids will be happy to do it if it means getting our school back again."

"I don't agree," Kim protested. "We like to use the playground equipment, too, and I for one am not willing to give it up."

"Actually, we won't have to give it up," I said. "I'm sure somebody will replace it. I mean, after all, who ever heard of a playground without playground equipment?"

"Who's going to spend money for that?"

"The PTA," I said proudly. "Don't you remember that meeting we went to?"

A light went on in Kim's head. "Oh, yeah! They said they wanted to replace the old playground equipment with some new playground equipment."

"Well, why can't we have the new playground equipment?" Kathy demanded. "Why do we have to have the old stuff?"

"Don't push it," Jonathan said.

"I think this is a great idea," Mack said. "Now if we can just keep Latham from causing problems, we'll be all right."

"Oh, don't worry about that," Mack said. He held up a padlock. "I'll just lock him in his casket for a few days and he'll cool down."

I had to laugh at that one.

"What do we do first?" Jonathan asked.

"I'll meet with some live kids at school in the morning, and we'll get up a task force to take down the playground equipment piece by piece and carry it all to the cemetery."

"Won't it be heavy?"

"Not if we carry it piece by piece. Anyway, we'll have most of the kids in the school to help us, so it shouldn't really take that much time."

The dead kids stood up.

"We need to get back to the cemetery before our parents leave," Kathy said. She turned to me. "Should we go to school today?"

I nodded. "Yes. We don't want anybody to know that we're planning to do something." I turned to Mack. "Are you sure you can keep Latham quiet about this?"

"I can take care of Latham," Mack said.

"I'll walk with you as far as my house," Kim said.

That surprised me. Before now, she'd always seemed a little afraid of the dead kids, but now she probably realized that they were just like she was except they were dead.

I walked downstairs with them.

"Will you be all right?" I whispered to Kim.

She nodded. Then she grabbed Kathy's bony hand. I had the feeling that they could once have been the best of friends.

I watched until I couldn't see them any longer.

Then I went back upstairs. Jonathan was still lying on the bed. I had to get some sleep, but I still didn't like the idea of sleeping with a dead kid, no matter how nice he was.

"I think I'll sleep downstairs on the sofa," I said. "I don't want you to be uncomfortable. That way you can stretch out."

"I hate to put you out," Jonathan said.

"I don't mind," I said, as I grabbed my pillow and took an extra blanket off the shelf in my closet. "I'll try to leave the house after Mom and Dad are gone. That way I won't have to do any explaining."

"Sounds good to me," Jonathan said.

I left my room and went back downstairs. If all goes well, I thought, we'll move the playground equipment to the cemetery tomorrow night and then maybe things will get back to normal. I grinned. I could hardly wait until the morning after, when Mr. Crabtree would see the empty playground.

"Who did this?" I was sure he'd ask me.

I already had my answer ready. "The dead kid!" I would reply.

I was sure that would finally make him rebury Jonathan so our lives would get back to normal.

12

I got to school early the next morning. Mack told me that he and the rest of the dead kids who had been in my room last night had talked to all the other dead kids, and they had all agreed that if they had playground equipment underground in the cemetery, they'd be perfectly happy to stay away from school.

So I spent the rest of the time before the first bell rang lining up kids to help me take the playground equipment apart piece by piece and move it to the cemetery that night.

By the time the first bell rang, I had signed up all of the sixth grade boys and girls.

"Man, I'm glad you thought of something to solve this problem," Ben told me, as we were walking into the building together. "I was getting tired of having to compete with those dead kids on the football field. I mean, next year, when I get to junior high, I want to start, but there were too many dead kids who were better than me."

I knew what he meant. I mean, when you think you're good at something, it's a real letdown to realize that someone who's dead is better.

Now that I finally had a solution to our problem, I was even able to pay attention in class.

During lunch, I signed up most of the boys and some of the girls from the fifth grade. I didn't bother with the fourth graders. I didn't think we'd need them, for one thing. I also thought they'd have a harder time slipping out of their houses at night. I remembered what it was like when I was in the fourth grade. Mom really checked on me. When I went into the fifth, she started worrying less and less about me and now that I'm in the sixth, she hardly worries at all.

I could hardly wait until I got home to tell Jonathan how great things had been. He hadn't come to school today, because the dead adults were still looking for him.

But as soon as I opened the door to my room, I knew something was wrong.

"This isn't going to work," he said.

I looked at him. "What do you mean? I've got it all planned. I have the kids lined up to move the playground equipment. The dead kids think that if they stay home all the time, their parents

127

will, too. It's got to work. I hate to tell you this, Jonathan, but everyone is getting really sick of having to compete with dead people!"

Jonathan grinned. "It's because we're better, isn't it?"

I didn't say anything.

"You don't have to say anything, Dunning. I know it is. Dead people always beat out live people."

"Okay, okay, I guess that in some things dead kids are better. So why won't it work?"

"There have been dead adults in and out of your house all morning, talking to your father about what they want. I don't think the dead adults are going to cooperate."

"What do they want?"

"They want their jobs back. They're bored playing cards all day in their caskets."

"I thought you said they weren't bored."

"I was wrong. I was thinking about my generation. It's these people who've only been dead less than twenty-five years. They're not satisfied with the way it's always been. They want to change things."

"Jonathan, the live adults are never going to let the dead adults move into their houses and take over their jobs. It's just not going to happen."

128

"Oh, it'll happen all right, Dunning, unless we can come up with a way to change their minds."

I lay down on the bed next to Jonathan. "I just need to think about it. There has to be a solution."

"I've been thinking about it all day, Dunning, and I still haven't come up with anything, so what makes you think you can?"

"The dead kids want playground equipment, so we're taking it apart and moving it to the cemetery tonight. The dead adults want houses to live in and stores to work in, so why can't we do the same thing?"

"You mean take apart all of the stores in Belton and move them to the cemetery?"

I shook my head. "I was thinking more along the lines of getting the lumber and stuff and letting the dead people build their own stores."

Jonathan thought for a minute. "You know, that might not be a bad idea. I'm sure that somewhere in the cemetery, there are dead carpenters, electricians, plumbers, and whoever else you need to build buildings."

"There have to be," I said.

"Why don't we start . . ."

I raised my hand to interrupt him. "I think we need to move the playground equipment first. I think we need to prove that it can be done. People

129

are going to think this is a crazy idea, anyway, so we have to prove to them that it'll work."

"You're right," Jonathan said.

I stayed in my room until Mom and Dad got in. Then I went downstairs, just to see if I could pick up some more about what was going on.

"It's terrible," Mom said. "These dead people have gotten so pushy."

Dad shook his head. "You can't talk to them, dear. They've already decided what they want to do, and they won't listen to reason."

"What are we going to do?" Mom asked.

Dad shook his head again. "We're still thinking, but everywhere we turn there's a dead person, so it's hard to get anything done."

Mom stood up and went to the kitchen. "I need to start dinner. I haven't eaten all day."

"I'll help you, Mom," I said.

Dad followed us into the kitchen. "At least the dead people don't just want us to pack up and leave," he said. "They've all agreed that they need our expertise—at least until they know what's going on."

"You know they'll pick our brains and then kick us out, don't you? That's what'll happen." Mom opened a cabinet door and then slammed it. "I've been so upset about all of this that I've forgotten to go to the grocery store. What are we going to eat?"

"Soup?" I suggested.

Mom looked at Dad. "That's about all I could eat, anyway."

So that's what we had.

I sat around with them for a couple of hours, while they watched television, and then I went to my room.

Jonathan was still lying on the bed. "It's not going very well, is it?"

I shook my head. "The dead adults are really being demanding. My dad thinks they may get violent."

"It could happen. I mean, they've been dead for a long time. There's probably a lot of pent-up hostility in them. They probably didn't want to die. They've just been waiting for a reason to come back and take what they feel is still rightfully theirs."

"This doesn't make sense, Jonathan. You mean that from now on people all over the world will have to be afraid of taking jobs or moving into houses that once belonged to dead people, because these people might come back one day and demand them back?"

"That's exactly what I mean. If we don't stop

131

this, then once the dead people of other towns learn what the dead people of Belton did, there'll be no stopping them."

I shivered. It was hard to imagine all the dead people who had ever died in the history of the world coming back to demand what was originally theirs. There'd be no end to it.

I looked at my watch. It was only ten o'clock. I had about two hours before I was supposed to meet all the other kids at the school, but I didn't think I could stand just sitting here. If we didn't move that playground equipment tonight, if we didn't do something to make the dead kids and the dead adults return to the Belton Cemetery, then this would be the end of the world as we knew it.

"I'm going," I said.

"Won't your parents know you're gone?"

"That's where you come in."

Jonathan just looked at me. "What do you mean?"

"I'm going to slip out the window. It's easy. I did it when I was a kid. My parents normally won't even come up here, but if they do, then you have to pretend you're me and disguise your voice. You can say something like, 'I'm already in bed, Mom, so thanks, but I don't need a glass of water.' "

"I hope I can remember that."

"It doesn't have to be that exactly, Jonathan, just a reference to whatever Mom is talking about if she says something, which she probably won't, but just in case she does, I want you to be prepared. I don't want her opening my door and seeing a skeleton lying on my bed. She probably wouldn't be able to take it." I looked at Jonathan and wondered if I had hurt his feelings. "No offense," I added quickly.

"None taken," Jonathan said. "You have to realize that dead people feel the same way about live people. They don't particularly like to be around them."

"Oh. No. I didn't know that."

"Yes, Dunning. It works both ways."

I put on my jacket and went over to the window. "I told all the other kids to bring screwdrivers and pliers and wrenches and things like that. Dad's are in our garage." I pushed the window open. "Wish me luck."

"Good luck," Jonathan said.

Then I climbed out.

I was amazed at how easy it was, swinging down from the limbs outside my window. I was only three feet above the ground when I jumped, so I landed without any problems.

Our garage is detached from our house, which

made it easy to get Dad's tools without his knowing it. I took what I needed, grabbed a flashlight, and headed down the street toward the elementary school.

I was surprised that three of the sixth grade boys and two of the fifth grade girls were already there. They said they couldn't stand waiting for midnight, either, so they came to the school. We decided that we could go ahead and start taking apart some of the playground equipment, because we'd probably need all of the time to get it moved before dawn.

The screws and the nuts and the bolts were all pretty rusty, but Collin Cutty had brought some kind of spray that almost melted the rust and made it easy to unscrew everything.

By midnight, as far as I could tell, everyone who had agreed to come had arrived, so it didn't take us long to take down the whole playground.

Actually, I was amazed. We were like ants at a picnic, attacking something and then carrying it away.

It occurred to me that we could probably do this to other things, if we had enough kids and enough tools. There was no telling what we could make disappear just by showing up late at night, taking it apart, and carrying it off.

Finally, around two o'clock, we had everything

disassembled and stacked at the edge of the playground.

Nobody had driven by to ask what we were doing. Of course, it helped that the playground was on the other side of the school, away from the street, so we couldn't be seen anyway.

"It's time to go to the cemetery now," I told everybody.

We had already made lists of the various parts of the playground equipment and who would be carrying what, so I simply called out the names as I stood by the parts. The kids came forward, lifted them, and started walking toward the cemetery.

This would be the hard part, I knew, because we had to walk down a couple of streets between the school and the cemetery, under streetlights. There was a good chance that someone who couldn't sleep would be up and looking out a window and see all these kids carrying disassembled playground equipment and have enough presence of mind to call the Chief of Police.

We were hoping this wouldn't happen, though, so we decided there wasn't much sense in having a backup plan in case it occurred. We'd just come clean and plead our case.

Finally, there were only two people left: me and

Kim, so we picked up part of the slide and started toward the cemetery.

The line kept moving, so I knew that nobody had stopped us.

Still, when Kim and I reached the two streets, I held my breath until we were on the back road to the cemetery. I didn't really breathe all that easy until we reached the cemetery.

The dead kids were waiting for us. I could tell that they were excited. They assured us that their parents were all busy playing cards and wouldn't notice us.

"The rest of you need to go home now," I said to the live kids. "When you come to school in the morning, act totally surprised and disappointed that the playground equipment has disappeared."

They all agreed that they would do a good job.

I had told the dead kids that Kim and I would help them reassemble the playground equipment under the cemetery.

The secret underground entrance was actually on the other side of the chain-link fence. It was under a scraggly bush and was just barely big enough for us to get all the equipment through, but, with the help of all the dead kids, we made it and stacked the equipment at the edge of the huge underground room.

As each piece of the playground equipment was

136

assembled, we lost some of our helpers to it. They would start swinging or sliding or riding the merry-go-round.

Finally, it was all reassembled.

I looked at my watch. "It's almost dawn," I said to Kim. "We have to leave."

We said good-bye to the dead kids, but most of them were too busy playing with the playground equipment to notice that we were leaving.

When we crawled out of the tunnel underneath the bush, the eastern horizon was a pale pink.

"We need to hurry," I said.

By the time I got home, it was almost light.

"How did it go?" Jonathan asked.

"Fine. The dead kids are happy."

"Do the dead adults know about it yet?"

"I don't think so."

"Then it's still dangerous."

I nodded.

I took a quick shower, then dressed and went downstairs. I told Mom I had gotten up early to study. She was still so upset by what was happening that I could have told her anything and it probably wouldn't have mattered.

I could hardly wait to get to school to see what happened.

Even though I was early, Mr. Crabtree and some of the other teachers were on the playground, looking stunned, wondering, I was sure, what had happened to the playground equipment.

When Mr. Crabtree saw me, he came running over. "Do you know anything about this, Dunning Healy?" he demanded.

This was the moment I had been waiting for. "Yes, sir, I do."

He just looked at me with narrowed eyes. When I didn't say anything else, he said, "Well? Who stole the playground equipment?"

"The dead kid did it!"

Mr. Crabtree just looked at me. "Which dead kid? We've got dead kids all over this school."

"Jonathan. The dead kid who's been living behind my locker. The one I asked you to rebury in the new cemetery."

"I will not be blackmailed," Mr. Crabtree said. "Besides, the School Board won't let me bury him."

I shrugged. Then I looked around the building. "Jonathan said he wouldn't mind taking this whole building."

"Taking it *where?*" Mr. Crabtree demanded. "Where would he take a whole building and how would he get it there? This isn't making any sense, Healy."

"You'll have to talk to him about that," I said.

"I refuse to negotiate with a dead kid. I refuse to do it."

I shrugged again.

The bell rang, so we all headed for the front door. Mr. Crabtree just stood where he was, probably trying to figure out what to do next.

There were no dead kids in classes today. Those of us who had moved the playground equipment to the cemetery had made a pact that we wouldn't tell anybody about it, but you know how that goes. Somebody had told a third and a fourth grader and they were blabbing it all over the place. Fortunately, none of the teachers believed them.

The main topic of conversation revolved around what we were going to do during recess.

As it turned out, we all just sat around on the ground and complained about not having any playground equipment.

"Maybe we should have kept it," David Wilson complained. "At least it was better than nothing."

"Yeah!" Carly Fortier agreed. "I mean, it's kind of dumb that we're just sitting around doing nothing at recess while all those dead kids are having so much fun."

"Be patient," I told them all. "Just be patient."

"We're trying," Kim said.

"If my plan works, then it won't be long until we have brand new playground equipment."

It didn't take long for something to happen.

140

Suddenly, there were live adults all over our playground, looking intently at the ground, trying, I suppose, to find holes where the playground equipment had sunk into the earth.

Several times, Kim punched me. "They'll never find it," she said gleefully.

I nodded.

Then the live adults were all inside the building, looking in all the rooms.

Once, I heard Mr. Crabtree say, "It's not here, I tell you. It just disappeared last night. The dead kid took it."

"Which dead kid?" one of the adults said. "You've had dead kids all over this school."

"Yes!" another school board member said. "It hasn't been pretty here."

Mr. Crabtree looked nonplussed. "What do you mean?"

"You're the only school in town with a dead kid problem, Crabtree. We thought you'd be able to solve it by now. You don't seem to be up to the task in elementary school, either."

"You're being considered for a demotion."

"Uh, uh, uh, uh," Mr. Crabtree tried to say, but the school board members stalked out of the building.

Actually, I had begun to feel sorry for Mr.

141

Crabtree. "Ms. Kienzle, Kim and I need to talk to Mr. Crabtree."

She just nodded. Her eyes were puffy from crying so much, I could tell.

Kim and I stepped out into the hall. Mr. Crabtree had started walking slowly toward his office.

"Mr. Crabtree!" I called.

Mr. Crabtree whirled around. "What do you want now?"

"You can solve this problem, sir," I said. "It's easy."

He raised an eyebrow. "Easy? Why should you want to make life easy for me?"

"If I make life easier for you, I'll make it easier for me and the rest of the kids at school."

Mr. Crabtree let out a big sigh. "Okay. I give up. I'll listen. The School Board's about to demote me, anyway, so what do I care? What do we have to do to solve this mess?"

"We rebury Jonathan in the new cemetery and then we ask the PTA to buy new playground equipment."

"If you'll remember, that's what they wanted to do with the money raised from selling candy bars," Kim said, "but you wanted computers, so it really shouldn't be a problem."

Mr. Crabtree thought for several minutes, then

142

sighed again. He knew it was out of his hands, that he had to do what we were telling him to do, so he threw up his hands and said, "All right! All right!"

"I'll tell Jonathan," I said.

"You do that," Mr. Crabtree said. He started to turn away.

"It'll mean digging up Mrs. Gillingham's fifth grade classroom," I pointed out.

"Okay. I'll call a man I know who has a jackhammer."

"We'll need a funeral home, too," I added.

Mr. Crabtree just looked at me. "I have this wonderful idea, Dunning. Why don't you just take care of all of this and I'll just go into my office and not come out until it's all over?"

"Okay, Mr. Crabtree. I'll do it."

I'm not sure if he thought I was kidding or not, but I went ahead as if he were serious.

I contacted the local funeral home and told them we were going to rebury a body that had been left behind when the cemetery had been moved.

At first, they were hesitant, so we called Mr. Crabtree, and when he got on the line, he said, "Hank, it's a long story. You see, we've got this dead kid who's causing a lot of trouble, because he wants to be reburied with his parents."

He listened for several minutes.

"I don't care what kind of orders you have to get, Hank. Look, the kid's been dead for fifty years, so why can't you just do it and not worry about getting permission? Who's around to give you permission anyway?"

Hank from the funeral home said he'd take care of it. He'd even take care of getting the man with a jackhammer to dig up Mrs. Gillingham's fifth grade classroom.

When school was out that day, I raced home. Neither Mom nor Dad was there, so I raced up to my room. Jonathan was lying on the bed watching television. When I told him that everything was set for the reburial, he said, "Good," but he never took his eyes off the television screen.

He was beginning to make me a little nervous, because if he changed his mind about wanting to be reburied and decided to stay with me, I didn't know what I was going to do. It's not the easiest thing in the world to get rid of a dead kid in your house, I was learning!

The next day was Saturday, so all the people from the funeral home, including the man with the jackhammer, met me and Kim and Mr. Crabtree at the school at six o'clock in the morning.

"I want this over and done with in one day," Mr. Crabtree said.

144

"You're paying," Hank said.

Jonathan hadn't wanted to miss the Saturday morning cartoons, so I didn't force the issue and left the house without him, but I told him I wanted him in his casket by noon. I didn't think they'd get through the floor before then, so I thought that would be enough time.

By eleven o'clock, however, the man with the jackhammer had made enough progress that I was afraid he'd reach Jonathan's casket earlier than I had thought. The men holding the rope hooks used to pick up the casket were already standing ready.

"Come with me," I whispered to Kim. "There are some loose ends we need to take care of."

We slipped out of the room and ran down the hall to my locker.

I opened the door and pushed the back away. "We have to make sure Jonathan's in his casket, because if he's not, we're in trouble."

"Yeah. Mr. Crabtree will probably go berserk if they reach the casket and Jonathan's not in it."

"I should have brought him with me. I shouldn't have let him watch television. I think he's hooked."

We crawled through the tunnel and finally reached the cemetery. Kim shined her flashlight

145

around and found Jonathan's casket. It had been moved back to its original burial place.

"Let's hope he's inside," I said.

We hurried over to the casket.

Kim knocked. "Jonathan? Are you in there?"

Just then, the jackhammer broke through from above, and pieces of concrete began falling around us.

"Oh, Dunning, this is awful!" Kim knocked harder on the casket. "Jonathan, are you in there?"

"Yes!" came a muffled voice.

I breathed a sigh of relief. "They're just about ready to lift you out. Stay where you are. It won't be long until you're in the new cemetery with the rest of your family."

"Thanks, Dunning. Thanks, Kim."

We started away, but Jonathan said, "Dunning?"

"What?"

"I have a confession to make."

"Make it quick. We have to get back up to the fifth grade classroom."

The rope hooks were already being lowered.

"I took your television set."

"What?"

"I know I shouldn't have, but I did. The reception isn't very good, but I can still watch some of my soap operas. I just couldn't not know how they turned out."

146

I looked over at Kim. "My television set has a built-in battery pack."

"Let him keep it," she whispered.

"That's okay, Jonathan. Don't worry about it. I can buy another one."

"Thanks, Dunning. You're a real pal."

For good measure, Kim and I made sure the rope hooks were in place along the handles of the casket, then we raced for the edge of the cemetery and started crawling frantically through the tunnel to the back of my locker.

We climbed through the locker and then ran to Mrs. Gillingham's fifth grade classroom. Jonathan's casket was just coming up through the hole in the floor.

"You almost missed it," Mr. Crabtree said.

"We had some important business to take care of," I said.

Mr. Crabtree gave us a peculiar look but didn't say anything else.

Kim and I rode to the cemetery in the hearse carrying Jonathan. When we got there, I could see a couple of other men toward the back of the cemetery.

"That's where the rest of Jonathan's family is buried," I whispered to Kim.

She nodded.

When the driver stopped the hearse, I tapped lightly on the casket. "We're here."

"I'm kind of nervous," Jonathan whispered back.

"You'll be all right," Kim said.

The two men in front got out, opened the back doors, and lifted out the casket. Then they carried it over to where the other men were waiting.

Mr. Crabtree stayed in the other hearse. Frankly, I thought that was kind of tacky, but I decided not to press the issue.

The two men lowered Jonathan's casket into the new grave; then the two other men started shoveling in dirt.

Kim and I stayed there until they were finished. The hearse with Mr. Crabtree in it had already left.

"Could you take us home?" I asked the driver of the other hearse.

"Sure thing, kids," he said.

When we were on our way, I said to Kim, "It's going to take a while to get things back to normal around here."

Kim nodded. "I wonder just how long the dead kids will be satisfied with that used playground equipment."

"Who knows?" I said.

14

The rest of the year went very well.

The dead kids kept their word. In fact, we never saw them again, although from time to time when Kim and I rode our bicycles by the cemetery, we thought we heard squeals of laughter and just knew they were all swinging, sliding, or riding on the merry-go-round.

The dead adults finally decided to stay in the cemetery, too, but only after Jonathan drew up some plans to build a complete city (patterned on Belton) underneath the cemetery.

We got some really fabulous playground equipment, which made us live kids not even want to come in from recess.

The School Board evidently forgot about Mr. Crabtree's demotion, and he and Ms. Kienzle finally got married.

Slowly but surely, everybody began to forget all about the dead kids.

When one of the kids in the sixth grade moved just after Christmas, I asked Mr. Crabtree if I could trade lockers. He let me. In fact, he didn't even ask me why I wanted to trade, but I told him I wanted a locker closer to my classroom. I was sure he didn't believe me.

Then, one week before school was out, a new kid arrived at school.

Naturally, he was assigned my old locker.

I couldn't believe what happened the second day he was there.

We were having free-reading period, and this kid said that he'd forgotten his book, so *Mrs.* Crabtree let him go out to his locker.

Suddenly, he came running back to class, screaming, "I just opened my locker, and this dead kid tried to pull me inside."

Mrs. Crabtree turned to me.

I shrugged. I couldn't imagine what Jonathan was wanting now, but I didn't want to find out.

Did *The Dead Kid Did It*
make your hair stand on end?
If you want more, check out
the following teeth-chattering
selection from *Fly By Night*,
the new Avon Camelot Spinetingler
coming in July 1996.

Ty stood up to get some speed and rode toward the old stone house, following the dirt road as it curved around. He didn't want to run into Mrs. Crow again. He shook his head, thinking. He hadn't told his mother anything about her and he wasn't sure why. Maybe, he admitted to himself, he was afraid his mother wouldn't let him ride out here anymore if he had.

It wasn't like Mrs. Crow had done anything scary, Ty argued with himself. Maybe there wasn't anything wrong with her except that she wasn't used to having people around. Maybe Mrs. Crow was just a loner like he was.

A crow suddenly swooped close, so low that Ty felt the wind from its beating wings. Startled, he ducked, his right foot sliding off the pedal. For an instant, Ty thought he was going to be all right; then the bike bounced into a rut. He fell, coming off the bike as the front tire rose, then slammed back down. Ty hit the ground hard, skidding a little on the rough dirt. Pain seared his right elbow and both knees as he hit. The handlebars were suddenly right in front of his face and he closed his eyes as his cheek hit the chrome. A dull pain spread across his face. Then everything was calm.

For a few seconds, Ty lay still, breathing hard. Then he slowly sat up. He was all right except for skinned knees, a scraped elbow, and a bruise on his cheek. But he was angry. What a stupid wreck. He looked up. He wasn't close to the house yet. Mrs. Crow wouldn't see him.

Ty stood and pulled the bike upright. He was furious with himself. Every day he saw the crows sitting on the fences in Pleasant Hills, or perching in the trees looking down calmly as people passed close to them. Too close. He should be getting used to that by now. So why did he have to crash his bike when one of them flew over his head a little too low?

"You're hurt."

Ty whirled around. Mrs. Crow was standing in the center of the road, her hands on her hips.

"Where were you?" he demanded, too upset to be polite.

Mrs. Crow shook her head, waggling an index finger at him. "Where was I, when? An hour ago? When I was your age? Last Tuesday?"

Ty stared at her. She was wearing dark clothes again, like she had just been to a funeral, and the clunky, dull yellow shoes. Her eyes were intense, and she stared at his face. Uncomfortable, Ty glanced across the fence and looked at the gravestones. The white one was larger than the other two. As he watched, a crow flapped toward it, spreading its wings and tail to land, cawing. Ty looked back at Mrs. Crow. There had to be a path into the bushes close by. Did she just wait around all day for people to come past so she could act weird?

"You aren't usually this clumsy, are you?" She smiled at him.

Ty shook his head. "I guess I'll get going now," he said, trying to keep his voice polite. He took a step backward.

Mrs. Crow made an odd sound deep in her

throat and Ty stared at her. She was pretty old. Maybe she did just walk around all day waiting to run into someone to talk to. It was her land, after all. She could do whatever she wanted on it.

"Have you heard any . . . odd . . . stories lately?" Mrs. Crow asked suddenly, her voice low. Ty felt his eyes widen. He looked down quickly, hoping she hadn't noticed.

"You have?" Mrs. Crow asked quickly. She took a step toward him and Ty took another step back. His knees hurt and he wanted to get started toward home. Mrs. Crow was staring at him, an impatient look on her face.

Ty shook his head. "I don't know what you mean."

Mrs. Crow pointed a bony finger at him. "Liar."

Ty hesitated, remembering what Tina had told Shari. "My sister's friend said her couch was turned upside down," he finally said, feeling silly. Mrs. Crow listened to the whole stupid story with her head tilted, her dark shiny eyes glued to his.

When he was finished, Mrs. Crow laughed. "A couch. Incredible."

Ty bent his arms and the scraped skin burned as he turned the bike around. "I have to go home now."

"There aren't more stories?"

Ty shook his head and started to walk slowly, shoving his bike along.

"Wait," Mrs. Crow said from behind him.

"I'd better start home," Ty said again, walking a little faster.

"Let me help," Mrs. Crow offered.

Ty shook his head, but she was already beside him. Ty stepped away, unsettled by her closeness. Her clothing was made out of some stiff, rustling cloth and she smelled dusty, like old curtains.

"I really don't need help," Ty insisted, leaning forward to push the bike a little faster.

Moving incredibly fast for her age, Mrs. Crow got past him and stood again, her hands on her hips. He stared at her. He didn't know what to say. All he wanted to do was to go home.

"Wait," Mrs. Crow said in a quiet voice. "Home isn't as far away as you think it is. Look." She pointed.

Ty followed her gesture. On the side of the road without the iron fence, there was a tangle of brush and weeds almost as tall as he was. He looked back at her face. "I really do have to go now . . ."

"*Look,* Ty," Mrs. Crow ordered. He looked again. This time he saw what she was pointing at. There was a faint path running through the dense undergrowth. He looked back at her.

"Where does it lead?"

"Home. Didn't you hear what I said?" She gestured for him to step onto the path.

Ty shook his head, about to argue. Then Mrs.

Crow simply turned and led the way. He followed. But as he did, he stayed a little distance behind her. He didn't really think that a tiny elderly woman could be dangerous, but he wouldn't have believed that she could walk this fast either. He was having trouble keeping up. Her clothes rustled as she moved through the thickets, following the narrow path.

"There," she said after a few minutes. Ty leaned on his bike and stared. The path opened onto the curving paved road that bordered Pleasant Hills.

Mrs. Crow cackled, but softly this time. "Where you turn off, the roads look like they go in entirely different directions, but the dirt road angles back until it's almost parallel to the street. The path just connects the two." She turned. Ty nodded. Just then a sudden burst of rasping shrieks made him look up. A flock of glossy black crows was winging through the air above them. When he looked back down, Mrs. Crow was gone. He thought he caught a glimpse of her dark form through the bushes, but he wasn't sure. He shoved his bike the last few yards up the path and started home. His knees were beginning to ache as he limped along the shoulder of the paved road. Above his head, the crows wheeled in a circle, screaming and cawing.